DISCARD

# Read All About It!

## by Valerie Tripp

★ American Girl®

# Kit's Family and Friends

**Dad**
Kit's father, a businessman
facing hard times

**Mother**
Kit's mother, who keeps
the household running

**Charlie**
Kit's brother, who is 16 and
wants to go to college

**Uncle Hendrick**
Mother's wealthy and
disapproving uncle

**Stirling Howard**
A boy who moves
into Kit's house

**Mrs. Howard**
Mother's friend
from the garden club

**Ruthie Smithens**
Kit's best friend,
who likes fairy tales

**Roger**
A know-it-all boy
in Kit's class

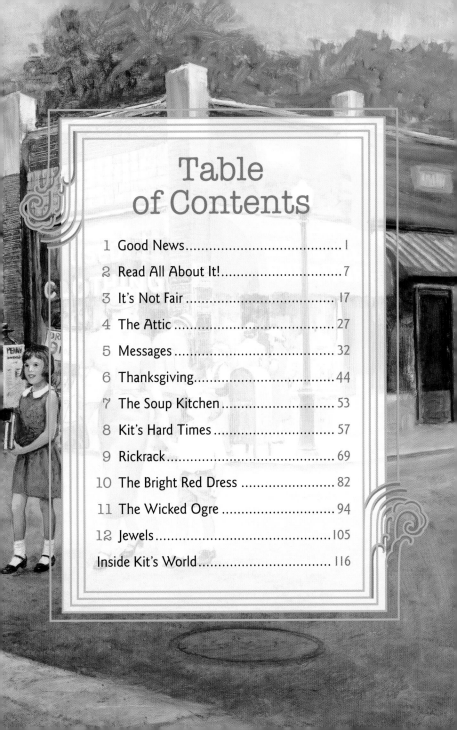

# Table
# of Contents

1 Good News.............................................. 1

2 Read All About It!................................7

3 It's Not Fair ....................................... 17

4 The Attic ........................................... 27

5 Messages ........................................... 32

6 Thanksgiving......................................44

7 The Soup Kitchen .............................. 53

8 Kit's Hard Times .............................. 57

9 Rickrack.............................................. 69

10 The Bright Red Dress ....................... 82

11 The Wicked Ogre ............................... 94

12 Jewels................................................105

Inside Kit's World................................. 116

# Good News

## CHAPTER 1

C lick, clack, clackety!
Kit Kittredge smiled as she typed. She loved the sound the typewriter keys made as they struck the paper and the *ping!* of the bell when she got to the end of a line. She loved the inky smell of the typewriter ribbon and the way the black letters looked as they marched across the page, telling a story the way *she* wanted it told.

It was a hot afternoon in August. Kit and her best friend, Ruthie, were in Kit's room writing a newspaper for Kit's dad. Every night when Dad came home from work, he gave Kit the real newspaper so that she could read the headlines and the baseball scores and the funnies. He was always very pleased when Kit gave him one of her newspapers in return.

Kit finished the paragraph she was typing about her brother Charlie, who was sixteen. "Read me what we have so far," said Ruthie.

Kit read:

```
      Congratulations to Charlie Kittreage!
He et set a World's Record today. He
ate A a Hole Kwhole plate of gingersnaps
that were supposed to be fore Mother's
garden club. Charlie is going to college
in a few weeks. He should try out for XX
the Eating Team!
```

Ruthie looked over Kit's shoulder and giggled as she read what Kit had written. "Now what?" she asked.

"I don't know," Kit sighed. "I wish something would happen around here. Some dramatic *change*. Then we'd have a headline that would really grab Dad's attention."

"Like in the real newspapers," said Ruthie.

"Exactly!" said Kit.

"Well," said Ruthie. "When my parents read the headlines these days, they get worried. The news is always about the Depression and it's always bad. I don't think we want our paper to be like that."

"No," said Kit. "We want *good* news."

She knew there hadn't been much good news in the real newspapers for a long time. The whole country was in a mess because of the Depression. Dad had explained it to her. About three years ago, people got nervous about their money and stopped buying as many things as they used to, so some stores had to close. The people who worked in the stores lost their jobs. Then the factories that made the things the stores used to sell had to close, so the factory workers lost their jobs, too. Pretty soon the people who'd lost their jobs had no money to pay their doctors or house painters or music teachers, so those people got poorer, too.

Kit was glad that her dad still had his job at his car dealership. She and Ruthie knew kids at school whose fathers had lost their jobs. They'd seen those fathers selling apples on street corners, trying to earn a few cents every day. Some kids had disappeared from school

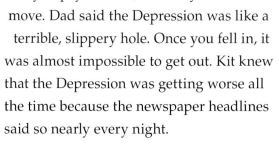

because their families no longer had enough money to pay the rent, and they had to move. Dad said the Depression was like a terrible, slippery hole. Once you fell in, it was almost impossible to get out. Kit knew that the Depression was getting worse all the time because the newspaper headlines said so nearly every night.

Just then, Charlie popped his head in the door. "Hey, girls," he said. "Mother's garden club's here. You better get downstairs quick if you want anything to eat. I saw Mrs. Culver already diving headfirst into the nut dish."

"Oh, boy!" said Ruthie. "Maybe there'll be some cake for us!"

"Maybe there'll be some *news* for us!" said Kit. "Come on, Ruthie!"

Kit and Ruthie thundered down the stairs. Kit's mother smiled when she saw the girls. Then she turned to her guests and said, "Ladies, you remember Ruth Ann Smithens and my daughter Kit, don't you?"

"Yes, of course!" said the ladies. "Hello, girls!"

"Hello," said Kit and Ruthie politely.

"Do help yourselves to some refreshments, girls," said Mother.

"We will!" said Kit and Ruthie, smiling broadly.

The girls filled their plates and retreated to a corner behind a potted palm to enjoy their feast and observe the ladies. At first the ladies discussed garden club business, such as how to get rid of bugs, slugs, and other garden pests. It was pretty boring, although the girls did get giggly when Mrs. Willmore said she was just beside herself because she had spots on her phlox.

Then the talk moved on to who was going to weed the flower bed at the hospital, which the garden club ladies took turns doing.

"I believe it is my turn," said Mrs. Howard. "But I'm afraid I won't be able to weed this month. In fact..." She hesitated, and blinked her big round eyes. "I'm afraid I won't be able to be part of the garden club at all anymore.

I'm moving to Chicago. My husband is already there, and so my son Stirling and I are going to join him. He's pursuing a business opportunity."

"Ahh!" said all the ladies brightly. They all knew what that meant. Kit did, too. It meant that Mr. Howard had gone to Chicago to look for a job. Everyone knew that Mr. Howard had not had a job for two years, ever since the company he worked for here in Cincinnati had gone out of business.

"Where will you live in Chicago?" one lady asked.

"I'm not sure yet," said Mrs. Howard, blinking again. "Mr. Howard hasn't settled anywhere. We'll be hither, thither, and yon for a while!"

The whole thing sounded pretty fishy to Kit. *If the Howards have no place to live in Chicago, why are they leaving their house in Cincinnati?* she wondered. Then suddenly, it dawned on her. The Howards *couldn't* stay in their house. They didn't have enough money. And Mr. Howard didn't have a job or a place for them to live in Chicago, either. That was the truth—Kit was sure of it. She was pretty sure that all the ladies knew it, too, but no one would say it out loud.

There was an awkward silence. Then Mother spoke up and made everything better. "I have a marvelous idea, Louise!" she said to Mrs. Howard. "We'd love it if you and dear Stirling would stay in our guest room until your husband is settled in Chicago and sends for you. Stirling is about Kit's age. I'm sure they'll get along beautifully."

"Well," said Mrs. Howard slowly. "If you're *sure* it isn't too much trouble, Stirling and I would love to stay. Thank you, Margaret."

"That's all settled, then," said Mother calmly.

All the ladies brightened up, as if a cloud had blown away. Kit started scribbling notes on her notepad, and Ruthie whispered to her, "Who's this boy Stirling?"

Kit shrugged. "He's Mrs. Howard's son, I guess," she said. "I haven't met him, but he's already done us a favor. Come on. I'll show you."

The two girls ran up the stairs to Kit's room. Kit stood in front of the typewriter. "Stirling's given us a headline," she said to Ruthie. "Look."

Kit typed in capital letters:

```
     THE HOWARDS ARE COMING!
```

# Read All About It!

## CHAPTER 2

**K**it's real name was Margaret Mildred Kittredge. She was named after her mother and an aunt of her dad's. But when she was very little, her dad used to sing her a song that went like this:

*Pack up your troubles in your old kit bag
and smile, boys, smile . . .*

It was a song he'd learned when he was a soldier fighting in the Great War. Kit loved it. She'd beg Dad, "Sing my song! Sing the kit song!" Pretty soon everyone began to call her Kit, which was also short for Kittredge, and the name stuck. Kit didn't like the name Margaret Mildred anyway. It didn't fit her. It was too flouncy. Kit was *not* a flouncy girl.

Kit was finishing her newspaper when she heard the car horn's cheery *honk-honk* that signaled her favorite moment of the day. Dad was home from work! Kit snatched up her newspaper, flew downstairs, and burst out the door, calling to Dad, "Look! I've got a newspaper for you today!"

"Oh ho," said Dad. His blue eyes were twinkly. He

smiled a broad smile as he took Kit's newspaper and handed her the real one. He read Kit's headline in a booming voice. "'The Howards Are Coming!'" Then he glanced at Kit and spoke in his normal voice. "Are they coming for dinner?"

"Nope!" said Kit. "They're coming to stay!"

Kit noticed, much to her surprise, that Dad's smile faded.

When Dad spoke his voice sounded funny, as if he was trying too hard to be hearty. "Well," he said. "That *is* big news! Come on, sweetheart. Let's go get the details from your mother."

*Grown-ups are funny*, Kit thought as she walked along next to Dad. *They don't react the way you expect them to.* Anyone would think that Dad was not pleased to have the Howards coming to stay. But why on earth wouldn't he be?

Two days later, Kit and Ruthie were sitting on the front steps waiting for Stirling and Mrs. Howard to arrive. Ruthie was reading *Beauty and the Beast*, and Kit was looking at the pictures in her book, *Robin Hood.*

Kit longed to sleep in a tree house high up near the sky, surrounded by leaves, like Robin Hood and his merry men did. She had spent many hours drawing plans for a tree house that she and Ruthie could build. Kit was not very good at sketching. Her drawings always looked like doghouses stuck up in trees. They didn't look anything like the tree houses in Sherwood Forest.

"I bet," said Kit, "that Stirling can help us build a tree house."

"Mmm," said Ruthie, with the tiniest hint of irritation at being interrupted when she was deep into the story of *Beauty and the Beast*.

It was hot, and the girls were licking chunks of ice that had been chipped off the big block of ice in the icebox. Kit's ice chunk had melted to a sliver when, at last, a cab pulled up to the end of the driveway. Kit and Ruthie stood up and waited politely on the front steps. The cab door opened, and Mrs. Howard and a boy got out. When she saw Stirling, Kit felt as if someone had dropped her ice chip down her back, she was so surprised.

Stirling stood next to the cab on two of the skinniest legs Kit had ever seen. He was short and pale and skinny all over. His head looked too big for his scrawny neck.

The screen door opened, and Mother came out of the house. She stood between Kit and Ruthie and put her hands on their shoulders.

"Mother!" whispered Kit indignantly. "Stirling's a shrimp!"

"Now, Kit," said Mother. "Stirling is small for his age because his health is delicate. But I'm sure he's a very pleasant fellow." Gently, she pushed the girls forward. "Come along, ladies," she said. "Let's go greet our guests and make them feel welcome."

Kit and Ruthie and Mother walked down the steps and toward the driveway. Mrs. Howard and the cab driver were unloading boxes and suitcases from the cab. Stirling just stood there.

"Oh!" said Mrs. Howard, all aflutter. "Margaret! You are such a dear to have us!" She turned to Stirling. "Shake hands with Mrs. Kittredge, lamby," she said. "And say hello to Kit and Ruthie."

Stirling shook Mother's hand and nodded at the girls. He looked even worse close-up. He had colorless hair, colorless eyes, and a red, runny nose. Kit towered over him, and Ruthie could have made two of him, he was so puny.

"Oh, dear!" fussed Mrs. Howard. "All this excitement is not good for Stirling, the poor lamb! He'll have to lie down right away and rest."

"Of course," said Mother. "Come with me and we'll get him settled."

Kit and Ruthie watched them go inside. "Well," said Kit. "*He's* a disappointment."

Ruthie shrugged. Then she said, "Of course in fairy

tales you learn not to judge by appearances. Lots of times perfectly nice people are under a spell."

But over the next few days, Kit's disappointment stayed. When she and Ruthie invited Stirling to run through the sprinkler with them, Mrs. Howard said, "Stirling can't get wet because he might catch a chill. And Stirling can't play in the yard because he's allergic to bee stings." Pretty soon, Kit abandoned any idea of Stirling helping with a tree house, and she gave up inviting him to do *anything*, because the answer was always "Stirling can't."

At first, Kit thought Mrs. Howard was making the whole thing up about how fragile Stirling was. It wasn't as if he had a sickness like rickets or scurvy or any of the really interesting diseases Kit knew about from reading pirate stories. Stirling didn't even have any spots or rashes. However, after he'd been at the Kittredges' house a week, Stirling got truly sick. Though it was only a cold, he did have a fever and a terrible cough. Mrs. Howard said that he had to stay in bed and have all his meals brought to him on a tray.

Kit could hear Stirling coughing and sniffling and blowing his nose all day long. Everyone had to tiptoe past the door to his room so they wouldn't disturb Stirling in case he was napping. Kit held her nose when she passed by, because the hall outside his room smelled strongly of

Vicks VapoRub even though the door was always shut.

But one afternoon, Kit noticed that the door to the guest room was open. She sneaked a peek inside. Stirling was propped up on the pillows, and Mrs. Howard was nowhere to be seen. Of course, it was hard to see *anything* in the room. It was dark because the shades were pulled down.

Kit stood in the doorway and looked at Stirling's moon-white face on the pillow. "Gosh, it sure is stuffy in here," Kit said to Stirling. "Don't you want me to open the window or something?"

Stirling nodded.

Kit opened the window a crack so that a breath of air and a thin line of sunlight came through. "That's better!" she said. Kit turned to go. She was halfway to the door when she saw a photograph next to Stirling's bed that stopped her in her tracks. "Hey!" she said. "Is that Ernie Lombardi, the catcher for the Reds?"

Stirling's round eyes were as unblinking as an owl's as he looked at Kit. His nose was stuffed up, so his voice sounded weirdly low and husky. "Schnozz," he croaked.

For a second, Kit didn't understand. Then she laughed and nodded. "Schnozz!" she said. "That's Ernie Lombardi's nickname because he has such a big nose."

In answer, Stirling blew *his* nose, which made a nice honking sound.

Kit laughed again. "Ernie Lombardi is my favorite player on the Cincinnati Reds," she said. "He's the reason I'm a catcher. Did you know that Ernie's the biggest guy on the Reds?"

"Six foot three," whispered Stirling hoarsely. "Two hundred and thirty pounds."

"Right!" said Kit, delighted. She rattled on. "It's funny that you like him," she said, "because he's so big and you're so little."

"That's why," said Stirling simply. He didn't sound the least bit offended, even though right after she spoke, Kit realized that she'd said something she shouldn't have.

"You know what?" said Kit, suddenly inspired. "I have a newspaper article about Ernie Lombardi. It has a photograph of him holding seven baseballs in one hand at the same time. It used to be tacked up on my wall. My mother wouldn't let me put it back up after my room was painted pink this summer, but I bet I can find it. Want to see it?"

Stirling nodded vigorously, and Kit noticed that his eyes weren't colorless at all. They were gray.

"Okay!" she said. "I'll get the article and you can read all about it!" Kit tore back to her room, rummaged through the drawers of her desk, and found the scrap of newspaper. She raced back to Stirling's room shouting, "I found it!"

Kit flung open the door and *BAM!* The door hit Mrs.

*"My land!" shrieked Mrs. Howard.*

Howard, who was standing right inside with a silver tray in her hands.

"*My land!*" shrieked Mrs. Howard. She lurched forward and the tray, which had one of Mother's best china teacups and saucers on it, went flying. The hot tea sloshed out all over the rug. The cup hit the floor and shattered, and the tray clanged to the ground with a noise like cymbals.

"Oh dear, oh *dear*!" fussed Mrs. Howard. At the same time, Stirling started to cough loudly. Kit tried to apologize in a voice louder than his coughs, and Charlie appeared and added to the commotion by asking, "What happened? What's all the noise?"

They were all talking at once when Mother came in. "Good gracious!" she said above all the racket. "*Now* what?"

Everyone stopped talking, even Mrs. Howard.

"Will someone please tell me what is going on?" asked Mother, not sounding at all like her usual serene self.

Everyone looked at Kit.

Kit knew that Mother disliked messes, so she tried to explain how this one was just an accident. "I was coming in here to show Stirling my picture of Ernie Lombardi," she said, "and I didn't know that Mrs. Howard was right behind the door. I was in a hurry and I—"

Mother held up her hand to stop Kit. "Don't tell me," she said. "I can imagine the rest." She shook her head.

"How many times have I told you to slow down and watch where you're going, Kit?"

"I'm sorry," said Kit.

Mother stooped down to pick up the broken cup. "Just look at what you've done," she said.

Kit was shocked. It wasn't like Mother to scold her so sharply. "But it wasn't *my* fault," she protested. "It was an accident. It was *nobody's* fault."

"Nobody's fault," repeated Mother. "And yet look at the mess we are in." She looked up at Kit. "Please go now," she said. "I'll help Mrs. Howard clean up. And Kit, dear, please don't barge in here bothering Stirling and making messes anymore."

"But I didn't—" Kit began.

"That's enough, Kit," said Mother. "Go now."

Kit gave up. She turned on her heel and stormed back to her room.

Kit rolled a piece of paper into the typewriter. In capital letters, she typed her headline:

# It's Not Fair

**P**ounding the typewriter keys as hard as she could made Kit feel better. The good thing about writing was that she got to tell the whole story without anyone interrupting or contradicting her. Kit was pleased with her article when it was finished. It explained exactly what had happened and how the teacup was broken. Then at the end it said:

> Sometimes a person is trying to do something nice for another person and it turns ᴋᴋᴋ out sadly badly by mistake. When ssomething bad happens and it isn't my anyone's fault, no one should be blamed. It's not fair!

Kit pulled her article out of the typewriter and marched outside to sit on the steps and wait for Dad to come home. She had not been waiting long before the screen door squeaked open and slammed shut behind her.

It was Charlie. He looked at Kit's newspaper and then said, "Listen, Kit. I wouldn't bother Dad with this today if I were you."

"Why not?" Kit asked.

Charlie glanced over his shoulder to be sure that no one except Kit would hear him. "You know how lots of people have lost their jobs because of the Depression, don't you?" he asked.

"Sure," said Kit. "Like Mr. Howard."

"Well," said Charlie, "yesterday Dad told Mother and me that he's closing down his car dealership and going out of business."

"*What?*" said Kit. She was horrified. "But . . ." she sputtered. "But *why?*"

"Why do you think?" said Charlie. "Because nobody has money to buy a car anymore. They haven't for a long time now."

"Well, how come Dad didn't say anything before this?" Kit asked.

"He didn't want us to worry," said Charlie. "And he kept hoping things would get better if he just hung on. He didn't even fire any of his salesmen. He used his own savings to keep paying their salaries."

"What's Dad going to do now?" asked Kit.

"I don't know," said Charlie. "I guess he'll look for

another job, though that's pretty hopeless these days."

Kit was sure that Charlie was wrong. "Anyone can see that Dad's smart and hardworking!" she said. "Plenty of people will be glad to hire him!"

Charlie shrugged. "There just aren't any jobs to be had. Why do you think people are going away?"

"Dad's not going to leave like Mr. Howard did!" said Kit, struck by that terrible thought. Then she was struck by another terrible thought. "We're not going to lose our house like the Howards, are we?"

"It'll be a struggle to keep it," said Charlie. "Dad told me that he and Mother don't own the house completely. They borrowed money from the bank to buy it, and they have to pay the bank back a little every month. It's called a mortgage. If they don't have enough money to pay the mortgage, the bank can take the house back."

"Well, the people at the bank won't just kick us out onto the street, will they?" asked Kit.

"Yes," said Charlie. "That's exactly what they'll do. You've seen those pictures in the newspapers of whole families and all their belongings out on the street with nowhere to go."

"That is not going to happen to us," said Kit fiercely. "It's *not.*"

"I hope not," said Charlie.

"Listen," said Kit. "How come Dad told Mother and *you* about losing his job, but not *me*?"

Charlie sighed a huge, sad sigh. "Dad told me," he said slowly, "because it means that I won't be able to go to college."

"Oh, Charlie!" wailed Kit, full of sympathy and misery. She knew that Charlie had been looking forward to college so much! And now he couldn't go. "That's terrible! That's awful! It's not *fair*."

Charlie grinned a cheerless grin and tapped one finger on Kit's newspaper. "That's your headline, isn't it?" he said. "These days a lot of things happen that aren't fair. There's no one to blame, and there's nothing that can be done about it."

At that moment, Kit felt an odd sensation. Things were happening so fast! It was as if a match had been struck inside her and a little flame was lit, burning like anger, flickering like fear. "Charlie," she asked. "What's going to happen to us?"

"I don't know," said Charlie. He stood up to go.

"Wait," said Kit. "How come you told me about Dad?"

"I told you because you're part of this family," said Charlie, "and I figured you deserve to know."

"Thanks, Charlie," said Kit. She was grateful to Charlie for treating her like a grown-up. "I'm glad you told me," she said, "even though I wish none of it were true."

"Me, too," said Charlie. "Me, too."

After Charlie left, Kit sat on the step thinking. No wonder Dad had not been happy about the Howards coming to stay. He must have been worried about more mouths to feed. And no wonder Mother had been short-tempered today. When she said that even though it was nobody's fault, they were still in a mess, she must have been thinking of Dad. It wasn't his fault that they'd fallen into the terrible, slippery hole of the Depression, and yet... it surely seemed as though they had.

The sun was setting, but it was still very hot outside. The air was so humid, the whole world looked blurry. Then, all too clearly, Kit saw a terrible sight. It was Dad. He was walking home. He did not see Kit yet, but she could see that he looked hot and tired. There was a discouraged droop to his shoulders that Kit had never seen before. It made Kit's heart twist with sorrow. For just the tiniest second, she did not want to face Dad. She knew that when she did, she'd have to face the truth of all that Charlie had told her. But Kit stood up and straightened her shoulders. Everything else in the whole world might change for Dad, but she wouldn't.

Kit ran to Dad the way she had done every other night

of her life when he came home. Dad caught her up and swung her around.

When he put her down, Kit looked Dad straight in the eye. "Charlie told me," she said. "Is it true?"

Dad knelt down so that his eyes were level with Kit's. "Yes," he said. "It is."

"Are we going to be all right?" Kit asked.

"I don't know," said Dad. "I truly don't know."

Kit threw her arms around Dad and hugged him hard. She crumpled up her newspaper in her fist behind Dad's back. Dad didn't need to read her newspaper. He knew all about things that were not fair.

By the time Kit went downstairs to breakfast the next morning, Dad had already left.

"He's gone to meet a business friend," said Mother.

"It'd be great if his friend offered Dad a job, wouldn't it?" said Kit.

"Yes," said Mother. "It would." She smiled, but it wasn't one of her *real* smiles.

Dad didn't get a job that day, or the day after that, or the day after that, though he certainly seemed to be trying. Every day he put on a good suit and rode the streetcar downtown. Every day he said he was going to have lunch

with a friend or a business acquaintance. Every day, Kit
hoped he'd come home with the good news of a new job.
But every afternoon, Dad came home tired and discouraged. All the bad news in the newspapers seemed to be
about Kit's own life now.

One afternoon after a week had passed, Kit and Mother
were on the back porch shelling peas when a huge black
car pulled up in the driveway.

"Oh, no," sighed Mother. "It's Uncle Hendrick." She took
off her apron and handed it and the peas to Kit. "Quick,"
she said. "Take these into the kitchen. And Kit, dear, while
you're in there, pour us some iced tea and bring it to the
terrace." Mother smoothed her hair, adjusted her smile, and
walked gracefully toward the car.

Kit was glad to escape inside. Uncle Hendrick was her
mother's uncle and the oldest relative Mother had left.
He was tall and gray, and he lived in a tall, gray house
near downtown Cincinnati. He always seemed to be in
a bad mood. *The last thing Uncle Hendrick needs is lemon,*
Kit thought as she put a slice in his glass. *He's already a
sourpuss.*

Kit put the iced tea on a tray and carried it to the
terrace. Mother was sitting on a wicker chair, but Uncle
Hendrick was pacing back and forth.

"Margaret," Uncle Hendrick said to Kit's mother. "If

you can't pay your mortgage, you'll lose this house. What are you going to do?"

"Well," said Mother, "we could . . . take in boarders. Paying guests. It's perfectly respectable. We'll take in teachers, or nurses from the hospital."

*Gosh!* thought Kit. *Would you listen to Mother!*

Uncle Hendrick harrumphed. "Well, Margaret," he said. "All I can say is that if my sister, your dear mother, could see you now, it would break her heart." With that, Uncle Hendrick strode back to his car and drove away.

Kit ventured out onto the terrace. "Are we really going to take in boarders?" she asked Mother.

Mother smiled, and this time it was one of her real smiles that made Kit feel like smiling, too. "I surprised myself by saying that," said Mother. "I'm afraid I just wanted to shock Uncle Hendrick. But I rather like the idea." Mother laughed. "Yes," she said. "I like the idea a lot. It was a brainstorm."

"What's Dad going to say?" asked Kit.

"That," said Mother, "is a good question."

Kit was not at all sure that she liked Mother's brainstorm. She wasn't crazy about the idea of strangers living in their house, especially considering the way Stirling had turned out. Kit could tell that Dad didn't like the idea either. Mother had first presented the idea to him in private, of course, before she spoke about it again at dinner that evening. Mrs. Howard was serving Stirling his dinner up in their room, so only the family was at the table.

"We have plenty of room," said Mother. "We should put it to use."

"I don't think it's necessary," said Dad. "I'm making every effort to find a job. Meanwhile—"

"Meanwhile this'll be a way for us to earn some money," said Mother.

Dad sighed. "I hate the idea of you waiting on other people, especially in our own home."

"We'll all chip in to help," answered Mother, in a way that made it clear that the question of taking in boarders was settled. Kit wasn't surprised. There was never any way to stop Mother once she'd made up her mind.

"But where will the boarders stay?" asked Kit.

"Charlie can move to the sleeping porch," said Mother, "and we can put someone in his room. I'm also planning to find two schoolteachers or nurses to share the guest room."

Kit perked up. "Does that mean that Stirling and his mother will be leaving?" she asked. That'd be *one* good thing about Mother's plan at least!

"They'll stay," said Mother. "They'll be paying guests from now on."

"But *where* will they stay?" asked Kit.

Mother looked at Kit and said calmly, "Stirling and his mother will move into your room."

"*Mine?*" asked Kit, in a shocked, squeaky voice.

"Yes," said Mother. "We need them. They've got to stay if we want to make enough money to pay the mortgage every month. I figured it out."

"But Mother!" exclaimed Kit. "Where will *I* sleep?"

"I was thinking," said Mother briskly, "that you could move up to the attic. There's plenty of room up there."

*The attic!* thought Kit indignantly. She was being exiled to the hot, stuffy attic so that sniffle-nose Stirling could move into *her* room with his hankies and his meals on trays and his Vicks VapoRub!

Oh, oh, *oh*! In Kit's mind she saw her headline again, in letters that were four inches tall:

# IT'S NOT FAIR!

# The Attic

## CHAPTER 4

**A**fter dinner, Kit climbed slowly up the stairs to the attic. She looked around at the lumpy, dusty piles that surrounded her. Then she sank down to the floor, overwhelmed by sadness. When she'd been wishing for change so that she could have a dramatic headline, she'd never imagined *this*! Terrible changes! And so many! And so fast! Dad had lost his job. She had lost her room. And in a way, they *were* going to lose their house. They'd still be living in it, but it wouldn't be the same when it was filled up with strangers. Nothing would *ever* be the same.

Kit almost never cried. She bit her lip now and fought back tears. Then, suddenly, Stirling's head appeared at the top of the stairs.

"What are you doing out of bed?" Kit asked, roughly brushing away a tear.

Kit could tell that Stirling knew she'd been crying, but all he said was, "I'm bringing this stuff from your room." He came all the way up the stairs and handed Kit a box.

Kit noticed that the photo of Ernie Lombardi, wrinkled but smoothed flat, was on top. "Thanks," said Kit.

"I brought you a tack, too," said Stirling. He gave Kit the tack and looked around. "I guess you can put Ernie Lombardi up anywhere you want to up here, can't you?" he said in his weirdly husky voice. Then he disappeared down the stairs.

After Stirling left, Kit looked down at the photograph. She felt oddly cheered to see it. *Old sniffle-nose Stirling is right,* she thought. *I guess I can put anything anywhere I want up here.*

Kit looked around the long, narrow attic. The ceiling was steeply pitched. There were regular windows at each end of the room, and dormer windows that jutted out of the roof and made little pointy-roofed alcoves, each one about as wide as Kit was tall. The windows went almost all the way to the floor of the alcoves. Kit managed to open one of the heavy windows. She knelt down, stuck her head out, and came face-to-face with a leafy tree branch.

At that moment, Kit got a funny excited feeling. Suddenly, she knew exactly what she wanted to do.

Over the next few days, Kit was glad that no one seemed to care what she was up to up in the attic. When she wasn't helping Mother downstairs, she hauled buckets of soapy water up there and scrubbed the windows till they sparkled. She swept the floor and pushed the boxes far to one end of the room. Finally the cleaning was done, and the fun part began.

In one alcove, Kit put a desk and a chair and her type-writer. That was her newspaper office alcove.

In another alcove, Kit tacked up her photo of Ernie Lombardi. On a nail, she hung her catcher's mitt. That was her baseball alcove.

In the third alcove, Kit made bookshelves out of boards and arranged all her books on them. She found a huge chair that was losing its stuffing, and she shoved it into the alcove and softened it with a pillow. That was her reading alcove.

The last alcove was Kit's favorite. She put a lumpy mattress on an old bed frame and pushed the bed into the alcove with the pillow near the window. She surrounded the bed with some of Mother's potted plants. That was her tree house alcove.

The very first night Kit slept in her tree house alcove, Mother came up to tuck her in. She sat on the edge of Kit's bed and looked around the attic.

"Well!" said Mother. "A place for every interest and every interest in its place. I can see that you've worked hard to make this attic your room. I'm proud of you, Kit."

"Thanks," said Kit.

"I'm sorry I haven't had time to help you," said Mother. "I'm afraid I've left you all on your own."

"That's okay," said Kit.

Mother kissed Kit's forehead. Then she picked up Kit's book. "Still reading *Robin Hood*?" she asked.

"Yup," said Kit. "*Robin Hood* gave me the idea to make a tree house alcove to sleep in." Kit also had plans for a swinging bridge to connect the window ledge to the tree just outside the window, but she didn't tell Mother. It was going to be a secret escape, like Robin Hood had.

"Good old Robin Hood," said Mother. "Robbing the rich to give to the poor."

Kit propped herself up on her elbows and looked at Mother. "Too bad there isn't any Robin Hood today," she said. "If rich people had to give some of their money to the poor, it would make the Depression better."

"It would help," said Mother. "But I don't think it would end the Depression."

"What will?" asked Kit.

"I don't know," said Mother. "Lots of things, I suppose. People will have to work hard. Use what they have. Face challenges. Stay hopeful." She looked around Kit's attic and smiled. "I guess they'll have to do sort of what you've done up here in your attic. They'll have to make changes and realize that changes can be good." Then she kissed Kit again. "Good night, dear," she said. "Don't read too late."

"I won't," said Kit. "Good night."

After Mother went downstairs, Kit flipped over onto her stomach and looked out the open window. She could hear the leaves rustling outside and see stars peeking through the branches. *Changes Can Be Good*," she thought. *That sounds like a headline to me.*

# Messages

## CHAPTER 5

**B**y the time school started in the fall, three new
boarders had moved into the Kittredges' house—
a musician named Mr. Peck and two young nurses, Miss
Hart and Miss Finney. The money they paid for their
rooms and meals helped Kit's family. Kit knew that was a
good change.

But with the new boarders plus Mrs. Howard and
Stirling, the house felt much too crowded. And Kit's list of
chores had gotten a whole lot longer, because all the extra
people meant more cooking, cleaning, and laundry. Those
were *not* good changes. It was almost a relief to head off to
school every morning.

*Almost*. On this rainy November morning, the attic
was cold, and Kit didn't want to get up. She shivered and
burrowed deeper under her covers.

"Hey, Kit, wake up."

Kit opened one eye and saw Charlie standing by her bed.
She put her pillow over her head and groaned, "Go *away*."

"Can't do that," said Charlie cheerfully. "Not till I'm
sure you're up and at 'em." He turned on the lamp. "Come

on, Squirt. Time to get to work."

Kit groaned again, but she sat up. "I'm awake," she yawned.

"Good," said Charlie. He tilted his head. "What's that funny sound?"

Kit listened. *Plink. Plinkplinkplink!* "Oh," she said. "The roof leaks."

"Why don't you ask Dad to fix it?" asked Charlie. "I'm sure he could."

"Well, it only leaks when it rains," said Kit.

"No kidding," said Charlie.

"Besides, I like the plinking sound," Kit said. "It's like someone's sending me a message in a secret code that uses plinks instead of dots and dashes." In adventure stories, people often sent messages in secret codes, and Kit was always on the lookout for excitement.

"*Plinkplinkplink,*" said Charlie. "That means 'Get up, Kit.'"

"Okay, okay!" laughed Kit as she got out of bed. "I get the message!"

"At last," said Charlie. "See you later." He waved and disappeared down the stairs. Charlie had to leave very early every day to get to his job loading newspapers onto trucks, but he always woke Kit and said good-bye before he left.

Kit dressed quickly. Mornings got off to a fast start at the Kittredge house these days. Mother was *very* particular about having breakfast ready on time for the boarders.

As Kit hurriedly tied her shoes, she saw that someone had moved her typewriter from one side of her desk to the other. *I bet Dad used my typewriter,* she thought. *He probably typed a letter to ask about a job.* Kit sighed. She promised herself that the day Dad got a new job, she'd make a newspaper with a huge headline that said, "Hurray for Dad! Bye-Bye, Boarders!" Kit could not *wait* for that day. She did not like having the boarders in the house *at all.*

The thought of that headline cheered Kit as she went downstairs to the second floor to face her morning chores. Her first stop was the bathroom, where she fished three of Dad's socks out of the laundry basket. Teetering first on one foot, then on the other, Kit put a sock over each shoe. She put the third sock over her right hand like a mitten. Then Kit propped the laundry basket against her hip and peeked out the door to be sure the coast was clear. It was. Kit took a running start, then *swoosh!* She skated down the hallway, dusting the floor with her sock-covered feet and giving the table in the hall a quick swipe with her sock-covered hand.

Kit skated fast. She could already hear the boarders rising and making the annoying noises they made every morning. As she skated past Mr. Peck's room, she heard him blowing his nose: *Honkhonk h-o-n-k! Honkhonk h-o-n-k!* It sounded to Kit like a goose honking the tune of "Jingle

Bells." The two lady boarders were chirping to each other
in twittery bursts of words and laughter. Next door to them,
in what used to be Kit's room, Mrs. Howard was bleating
and baaing over Stirling like a mother sheep over her lamb.
*A chirp, chirp here and a baa, baa there! It's like living on Old
MacDonald's Farm, for Pete's sake!* Kit thought crossly. She
skated to the top of the stairs, sat, peeled off the socks, and
put them back in the laundry basket. Then she climbed onto
the banister and polished it by sliding down it sideways.
She landed with a thud at the foot of the stairs and found a
surprise waiting for her: Mother.

"Oh! Good morning, Mother!" said Kit.

Mother crossed her arms over her chest. "Is that how you do your chores every day?" she asked. "Skating and sliding?"

"Uh . . . well, yes," said Kit.

"No wonder the hallway is always so dusty. Not to mention Dad's socks," said Mother. She sighed a sigh that sounded weary for so early in the morning. "Dear, I thought you understood that we've all got to work hard to make our boardinghouse a success. Your chores are not a game. Is that clear?"

"Yes, Mother," said Kit.

"I'd appreciate it if you would dust more carefully from now on," said Mother. She managed a small smile. "And so would Dad's socks."

Kit felt sheepish. "Should I dust the hall again now?" she asked.

"I'm afraid there's no time," said Mother. "I'll try to get to it myself later. Right now I need your help with break-fast. The boarders will be down any minute. Come along."

"Okay," Kit said as she followed Mother into the kitchen. To herself she groused, *The boarders! It's all their fault. Mother never scolded me about things like dusting before they came, because I never had boring chores to do!* Kit knew her skate-and-slide method of dusting was slapdash, but she'd thought that nobody had noticed the dust left in the

corners—except maybe persnickety Mrs. Howard. She
should've known Mother would see it, too.

Mother wanted everything to be as nice as possible for
the boarders. She insisted that the table be set beautifully
for every meal. She went to great pains to make the food
look nice, too, though there wasn't much of it. Dad went
downtown nearly every day and brought home a loaf of
bread and sometimes cans of fruits and vegetables. But
even so, Mother had to invent ways to stretch the food so
that there was enough. This morning Kit watched Mother
cut the toasted bread into pretty triangles. Then, after Kit
spooned oatmeal into a bowl, Mother put a thin slice of
canned peach on top.

"That looks nice," said Kit. "The toast does, too."

"Just some tricks I've learned," Mother said. "Cutting
the toast in triangles makes it look like there's more than
there really is. And I'm hoping the peach slices will distract
our guests from the fact that we've had oatmeal four times
this week already. But it's cheap and it's filling."

"Humph!" said Kit as she plopped oatmeal into another
bowl. "Oatmeal's good enough for *them*."

"Hush, Kit!" said Mother. She glanced at the door to
the dining room as if the boarders might have heard. "You
mustn't say that. We've got to keep our boarders happy. We
need them to stay. In fact, we need more."

"*More* boarders?" asked Kit, horrified. "Mother, why?"

"Because," said Mother, sounding weary again, "even with Charlie's earnings and the rent from the boarders, we don't have enough money to cover our expenses. We need at least two more boarders to make ends meet."

"But where would we put them?" asked Kit. "No one would pay to share my attic. The roof leaks! And Charlie's sleeping porch is going to be freezing cold this winter."

"Yes," agreed Mother. "The sleeping porch should be enclosed, but we don't have any money for lumber."

*sleeping porch*

"Anyway," said Kit, "it'd be silly to go changing the house all around and filling it with boarders when I bet Dad is going to get another job any day now. Didn't he say he's going downtown again today to have lunch with a business friend?"

"Mmmhmm," Mother murmured.

"Probably it's an interview!" said Kit. She crossed her fingers on both hands. "Oh, I hope Dad gets a job!" she wished aloud.

"That," said Mother, "would be a dream come true." She handed the heavy breakfast tray to Kit, took off her apron, and smoothed her hair. "Meanwhile, all we have going for us is this house and our own hard work. We must do everything we can to make sure our boarders stay. We can't let them see us worried and moping. So! Shoulders back, chin up, and put on a cheery morning face, please."

Kit forced her lips into a stiff smile.

"I guess that will have to do," said Mother briskly. She put on a smile too, pushed open the door, and walked into the dining room like an actress making an entrance on a stage. Dad and all the boarders were seated at the table. "Good morning, everyone!" Mother said.

"Good morning!" they all answered.

Kit's smile turned into a real one when she saw Dad, who was wearing his best suit and looking very handsome. He winked at her as if to send her a message that said, *It really **is** a good morning now that I've seen you.*

Miss Hart and Miss Finney cooed with pleasure when Kit set their peachy oatmeal before them. Kit was careful not to spill. Their starched nurses' uniforms were as white as blank pieces of paper before a story was written on them. *I bet Miss Hart and Miss Finney have plenty of interesting stories to tell about their patients at the hospital*, thought Kit. *Maybe they've had daring nursing adventures, like Florence Nightingale and Clara Barton. What great newspaper headlines those adventures would make!*

Then Kit scolded herself for being curious. Miss Hart and Miss Finney must remain blank pages! Kit did not want to like them. She did not want to be interested in them or in Mr. Peck, either, even though he played a double bass as big as a bear and had a beard and was so tall he reminded Kit of Little John in her favorite book, *Robin Hood*. They would probably all turn out to be dull anyway, just as disappointing as tidy Mrs. Howard and skinny Stirling. They were *not* friends. They were only boarders, and they wouldn't be around for very long. As soon as Dad got a new job, they'd leave. Kit thought back to the wish she'd made and rewrote it in her head. *I should have added the word **soon**,* she thought. *I hope Dad gets a job soon.*

As Kit sat down at her place, she saw Dad slip his toast onto Stirling's plate. Stirling's mother saw, too, and started to fuss. "Oh, Mr. Kittredge!" said Mrs. Howard to Dad. "You're too generous! And Stirling's digestion is so delicate! He can't eat so much breakfast. It's a shame to waste it."

"Don't worry, Mrs. Howard," joked Dad. "Stirling's just helping me be a member of the Clean Plate Club. I'm having lunch with a friend today. I don't want to ruin my appetite."

Stirling didn't say a word. But Kit noticed that he wolfed down his own toast and Dad's, too, pretty fast. *Delicate digestion, my eye,* thought Kit.

"Goodness, Mr. Kittredge," Miss Finney piped up. "Last night at dinner you said you weren't hungry because you'd had a big lunch. Those lunches must be feasts!"

"They are indeed," said Dad.

Just then, Mother brought in the morning mail. She handed a couple of letters to Dad and one fat envelope to Miss Hart, who got a letter from her boyfriend in Boston practically every day. Kit was trying to imagine what Miss Hart's boyfriend had to say to her in those long letters when Mother said, "Why, Stirling, dear, look! This letter is for you."

Everyone was quiet as Mother handed Stirling the letter. Even his mother was speechless for once. The tips of Stirling's ears turned as pink as boiled shrimp. He looked at the envelope with his name and address typed on it and then eagerly ripped it open, tearing it apart in his haste to get the letter out and read it.

Mrs. Howard recovered. "Who's it from, lamby?" she asked.

Stirling smiled a watery, timid-looking smile. "It's from Father," he answered. His odd husky voice sounded unsure, as if he himself could hardly believe what he was saying.

"My land!" exclaimed Mrs. Howard, pressing one hand against her heart. "A letter at last! What does he say?"

Stirling read the typewritten letter aloud. "'Dear Son, I haven't got a permanent address yet. I'll write to you when I do, and I'll send more money as soon as I can. Give my love to Mother. Love, Father.'" Stirling handed two ten-dollar bills to his mother. "He sent us this."

"Wow!" exclaimed Kit. "Twenty dollars? That's a lot of money!"

Miss Finney and Miss Hart murmured their agreement, and Mr. Peck put down his coffee cup in amazement.

Mrs. Howard was overcome with happiness. In a weak voice she said to Mother, "Margaret, take this." She tried to give Mother one of the ten-dollar bills. "You've been so kind to us. You must share in our lucky day."

"Oh, but—" Mother began.

"I insist," said Mrs. Howard.

Mother hesitated. Then she said, "Thank you." She put the ten-dollar bill in her pocket.

After that, everyone started talking at once about Stirling's startling letter. Everyone but Stirling, that is. Kit saw Stirling read his father's message once more and then fold the letter very small and hold it in his closed hand.

After breakfast, Dad sat at the kitchen table reading the want ads in the newspaper while Kit and Mother washed the dishes. "Mr. Howard must be doing all right if he can send his wife twenty dollars," Dad said. "Maybe Chicago is the place to go. Maybe there are jobs there."

"Chicago *is* a bigger city than Cincinnati," said Mother.

"We'd move to Chicago?" asked Kit. She didn't like the idea of leaving her home and her friends.

"No," said Dad, putting the newspaper down. "Only I would go."

Kit spun around from the sink so fast, she left a trail of soapsuds on the kitchen floor. "You'd go without us?" she asked, shocked. "You'd leave us? Oh, Dad, you can't!"

"Now Kit, calm down," said Dad. "It's just an idea. I haven't said I'll go. But if nothing turns up here by Thanksgiving—"

"Thanksgiving?" interrupted Kit. "That's only two weeks away!"

"You know how hard your father's been looking for a job here in Cincinnati," said Mother. "Ever since August."

"And he'll find one," said Kit. She looked at her father. "Won't you, Dad? One of those business friends you have lunch with is sure to offer you a job any day now, right?"

"Kit, sweetheart," Dad started to answer, then stopped. He picked up the paper and went back to his reading. "Right," he said. "Any day now."

As Kit turned back to the dishes, she thought, *When I wished for Dad to get a job soon, I didn't mean in Chicago!* In her head, she rewrote the message of her wish again. Now it was: *I hope Dad gets a job **soon**, and **here in Cincinnati**.*

# Thanksgiving

## CHAPTER 6

**A**t school that morning, Kit's teacher, Mr. Fisher, said, "Now, boys and girls, as you all know, Thanksgiving is coming soon. I'd like our class to do its part to help the hungry. So if you can, please bring in an item of food. It doesn't have to be anything big. An apple or a potato will do. I know most of us don't have much food to spare. But if we all chip in, we can make a Thanksgiving basket and donate it to a soup kitchen."

The students murmured among themselves, but without much enthusiasm. They'd all seen soup kitchens with long lines of people waiting outside them. Kit had once seen a man in a soup line faint on the street from hunger. She knew that soup kitchens were for people who had been without work for so long that they had no money or hope or pride left, and who were so desperate that they had to accept free food.

"My father says that people who go to soup kitchens should be ashamed," said a stout boy named Roger, full of bluster. "They're bums."

"They're not bums," said Ruthie. "Most of them are

perfectly nice, normal people who happen to be down on their luck. I think we should feel sorry for them."

"My father says they're just too lazy to work," said Roger. "And now that Franklin Roosevelt's been elected, people will expect the government to take care of them. My father says it'll ruin our country."

Kit grew hot under the collar listening to Roger and thinking of how hard Dad was trying to find a job. "People aren't too lazy to work," she said. "They'd work if they could find a job. But jobs are hard to find."

Mr. Fisher nodded. "These are hard times," he said.

"But Mr. Fisher," a girl named Mabel asked, "we're still going to have a Thanksgiving pageant this year, aren't we?"

"Yes, of course," said Mr. Fisher. "The sixth-graders will be the Pilgrims," he said. "The fifth-graders will be the Indians. Our fourth grade is responsible for the scenery." Mr. Fisher held up a drawing. "Here's a drawing of the backdrop we'll paint." The drawing showed four giant turkeys and a cornucopia with fruits and vegetables spilling out. The turkeys' feathers were different colors. They were made out of bits of paper cut to look like real feathers, and they were glued onto the turkeys.

"That's good!" said a boy named Tom.

"Yes, it is, isn't it?" said Mr. Fisher.

"Who drew it?" asked a girl named Dorothy.

"Stirling," said Mr. Fisher.

Everyone, including Kit, twisted around to stare at Stirling, gaping in astonishment.

At lunch Ruthie said, "I have some good news, Kit! There's some wood left over from our new garage. My father said that you and I can use it for our tree house."

"That's great!" said Kit. She knew her family had absolutely no money to spend on something as unnecessary as wood for a tree house. So it was lucky that Ruthie's father, who still had a job, was giving away the leftover wood.

"I was thinking," said Ruthie. "Your tree house sketches have never turned out very well. Why don't we ask Stirling to draw a plan for us?"

"No!" Kit said. "Gosh, Ruthie! If we let him plan a tree house for us, then when it's built he'll want to come in it and we'll have to let him. He's already invaded my real house. I don't want him in our tree house, too!"

"Okay, okay," said Ruthie. "Don't get all worked up. The tree house doesn't even *exist* yet!"

"I'll ask Dad to help us," said Kit. "He loves building things. How soon can we get that wood?"

A few days later, Kit's class was on the stage in the school auditorium working on the backdrop for the Thanksgiving pageant. Stirling had drawn the outline on big sheets of paper that were pinned to the curtains at the back of the stage. The boys in the class were painting in the fruits and vegetables and the cornucopia. The girls were cutting out paper turkey feathers. Stirling was standing on a stool, gluing the finished feathers onto the outlines of the giant turkeys.

Mr. Fisher was far away, up in the balcony wrestling with the spotlights, and Roger was taking advantage of his absence by being a general pain. He came over and jabbed Stirling with his paintbrush. "So, Stirling," he said, "when's the wedding for you and Kit?"

It was as if Stirling hadn't heard Roger. He stepped down off his stool and calmly began brushing glue onto another batch of turkey feathers.

Roger turned his back on Stirling. "Hey, Kit," he said. "What's the matter with your boyfriend? He's awful quiet."

"Stirling is *not* my boyfriend," snapped Kit. "He and his mother *pay* to live at our house. They're *boarders*."

"Oh yeah!" Roger drawled. "That's right." He plopped himself down on the stool that Stirling had been using. Loudly and slowly, so that everyone could hear him, Roger said, "I heard that your family is so hard up you're running a boardinghouse now." He smirked. "And *you're* the maid."

"I am not!" Kit denied hotly. Of course, she *had* been feeling like a maid lately. But she'd never give Roger satisfaction by admitting it.

"That's not what I heard," Roger taunted. "Here's you." He pretended that his paintbrush was a maid's feather duster and he used it to brush some imaginary dust off his arms. Then he stood up, turned, and started to swagger away.

It was then that Kit saw the giant turkey feathers stuck to the seat of Roger's pants! Kit touched Ruthie's arm and pointed at Roger.

Ruthie chortled when she saw the feathers. "Hey, look, everybody!" she called out gleefully, pointing to Roger's bottom. "Look at Roger— Mr. Turkey-pants!"

Everyone looked. The girls screamed with laughter and the boys whistled and clapped. "Hey, Turkey-pants!" Ruthie hooted. "Gobble, gobble!" Kit realized with surprise that Stirling must have sneaked the gluey feathers onto the stool just as Roger sat down so they'd stick to his pants when he stood up.

Roger also realized that Stirling was the one who'd tricked him. "You think you're pretty smart, don't you,

Stirling?" he said furiously as he pulled off the gluey feathers. "Sticking your stupid turkey feathers on me. Well, at least *my* father hasn't flown the coop and disappeared like yours has!"

By now the whole class was gathered around Kit, Ruthie, Stirling, and Roger. They all looked at Stirling, waiting to hear what he'd say to Roger.

But Stirling didn't say anything, and his silence exasperated Kit. "For your information, birdbrain," she said to Roger, "Stirling's father sent him a letter from Chicago just a few days ago." She paused for impact. "And it had twenty dollars in it! His mother gave ten dollars to my mother."

Everyone gasped. *"Twenty dollars!"* they whispered in amazement.

"Well," sneered Roger. "That's good news for *your* family then, Kit, since your father doesn't have a job *or* any money. My father says your dad used up all of his savings to pay the people who worked at his car dealership, which was stupid. No wonder no one will offer him a job."

"That's not true!" said Kit, outraged. "My father has job interviews all the time. Almost every day he has big, fancy lunches and meetings about jobs. He'll get one any day now. He said so."

"No, he won't," said Roger. "Nobody wants your father." With that, Roger shoved his armful of sticky turkey feathers at Kit, who shoved them right back. Kit was so angry and shoved so hard that Roger staggered backward, lost his balance, and fell against a ladder that had a bucket of white paint on it. Everyone shrieked in horror and delight as the can fell over, splattering white paint on the backdrop and clonking Roger on the head! White paint spilled over Roger's hair and face and shoulders and back and arms. It ran in rivers down Roger, striping his legs and his socks and pooling into white puddles around his shoes.

"Arrgghh!" Roger roared. He swiped his hand across his face to clear the paint out of his eyes and lunged for Kit.

But at that very instant, Mr. Fisher appeared and shouted, *"Stop!"*

Roger stopped. Everyone was quiet.

Mr. Fisher frowned as he surveyed the white mess. "Who's responsible for this?" he demanded.

"Not me!" said Roger. "Stirling started it. He stuck feathers on me. And then Ruthie called me Mr. Tur—a stupid name—and Kit shoved me into the ladder. *They* did it, not me. They—"

Mr. Fisher held up his hand. "Quiet," he said. "Roger, go to the boys' room and clean yourself up. Boys and girls, I want you to go back to the classroom and sit silently at your desks. Kit, Ruthie, and Stirling, you three stay here. I want to talk to you."

Roger scuttled past Kit on his way out. "*Now* you're going to get it," he hissed at her, sounding pleased. "*Now* you'll be sorry!"

Kit lifted her chin. "I'm not sorry I shoved you, Roger," she said. "I'd do it again, no matter what the punishment is. I'd shove anyone who says anything mean about my dad!"

"So watch out!" added Ruthie for good measure.

Roger made a face. But for once, he made no smart remark in reply.

When Kit, Ruthie, and Stirling were walking home from school later, the girls agreed that Mr. Fisher's punishment was not too terrible, really. They'd had to clean up the stage, and they were going to have to spend their recess time for the rest of the week helping Stirling redo the backdrop where white paint had spattered on it. Mr. Fisher had also decided that Kit, Ruthie, and Stirling would deliver the class's Thanksgiving basket to a soup kitchen while the rest of the class was watching the Thanksgiving pageant.

"The only bad part of the punishment is missing the pageant," said Ruthie. "Especially because we have to go to a soup kitchen instead."

"The worst part to me is that loudmouth Roger isn't being punished," said Kit. "It's not fair. He's the one who started the whole fight."

"Don't worry," said Ruthie. "In fairy tales, bad guys like Roger always get their comeuppance in the end. Everyone finds out the truth eventually."

That reminded Kit of something. "Uh, Stirling," she said. "It would probably be better if we didn't say anything about this . . . this situation when we get home. My mother might get a little upset if she found out."

"Mine, too," said Stirling. His voice was serious, but Kit saw a little ghost of a smile flicker across his face. She understood. They both knew that Stirling's mother would go into absolute *fits* if she found out her little lamb had been involved in a fight. And she'd surely come swooping down to school and insist that he couldn't possibly go to a soup kitchen. Think of the germs!

"You know, Stirling," said Ruthie, "I think you're being pretty nice about this whole thing. After all, it was your drawing that was ruined by all that paint."

Another smile flickered across Stirling's face. "Too bad the first Thanksgiving didn't take place during a blizzard," he said in his low voice. "Then Roger could have been the Abominable Snowman in the pageant."

Ruthie laughed. And Kit did, too.

# The Soup Kitchen

## CHAPTER 7

**S**tirling knew how to keep quiet. He did not spill the beans about the spilled paint, the fight, or the punishment. So when the day came for the trip to the soup kitchen, Kit and Stirling went off to school as if it were a normal morning. They did bring Kit's wagon with them, but the grown-ups were too busy to notice.

After an early lunch at school, the rest of the class went to the pageant. Mr. Fisher helped Kit, Ruthie, and Stirling put the Thanksgiving basket into the wagon. It was heavy. Students had brought potatoes, beans, and apples. There were a few jars of preserves and six loaves of bread. Kit and Stirling brought a can of fruit, and Ruthie, whose family still had plenty of money, brought in a turkey that weighed twenty pounds.

"The soup kitchen is down on River Street," said Mr. Fisher. "After you deliver the basket, you may go home." He paused. "Happy Thanksgiving," he said. Then he hurried off so he wouldn't miss the beginning of the pageant.

Kit, Ruthie, and Stirling set out. When they turned the corner onto River Street, they saw a line outside the soup kitchen. It was four people across, and it stretched from the door of the soup kitchen all the way to the end of the block. The people stood shoulder to shoulder, hunched against the rain. The brims of their hats were pulled low over their faces as if they were ashamed to be there and did not want to be recognized.

"Oh my," said Ruthie quietly.

Stirling said nothing, but he moved up to stand next to the girls.

Kit prided herself on being brave, but even she was daunted by the dreary scene before her. She squared her shoulders. "Let's go around to the back door," she suggested. "That's probably the right place to make a delivery."

Kit led the way down a small alley and around to the rear of the building. She knocked on the back door. No one answered. Kit lifted the basket out of the wagon. She took a deep breath, pushed the door open, and stepped inside. Stirling and Ruthie followed her. In the kitchen, people were rushing about with huge, steamy kettles of soup, trays of sandwiches, and pots of hot coffee. A swinging door separated the kitchen from the room where the food was served and the groceries were given away.

One lady saw Kit and the others and stopped short. She peered through the steam rising off the soup she carried and said, "Thank you for coming! You'll have to unpack the basket yourselves. Leave the turkey and the potatoes here in the kitchen. We'll use them to make tomorrow's soup. But bring the canned goods and the loaves of bread out front now. You can give them away."

Kit, Ruthie, and Stirling did as they were told. After they unloaded the basket, they pushed through the swinging door from the kitchen to the front room, which was crowded with people. It smelled of soup and coffee. At round tables in the center of the room, people sat eating and drinking. Some talked quietly. But most of the people kept a polite silence, as if they did not want to call attention to themselves or make themselves known to anyone around them. Along one side of the room, there was a long table with people lined up in front of it. Kit could see only their backs as they stood patiently, holding bowls and spoons, waiting for soup to be served to them. Across the room there was another long table where a lady was handing out groceries and loaves of bread for people to take home. Rather shyly, Kit, Ruthie, and Stirling went over, put their food on the table, and stood next to her.

"Thanks," said the lady. "Please give the bread to the people as they pass by."

Kit, Ruthie, and Stirling kept their eyes on the bread as they handed it out. It was kinder and more respectful not to look into the faces of the people, who seemed grateful but embarrassed to be accepting free food. Most of them kept their eyes down, too. Kit felt very, very sorry for them as they took their bread, murmured their thanks, and moved away. *All of these people have sad stories to tell*, she thought. *They weren't always hungry and hopeless like they are now. How humiliating this must be for them!*

The lady handing out the groceries seemed to know some of the people. "Well, hello!" she said to one man. "You're here a little later than usual today."

Kit handed the man his bread.

"Thank you," he said.

Kit looked up, bewildered.

It was Dad.

# Kit's Hard Times

## CHAPTER 8

**K**it!" Dad gasped.

Kit couldn't breathe. She felt as if she had been punched in the stomach. Shock, disbelief, and a sickening feeling of terrible shame shot through her as she stared at Dad.

Suddenly, Kit could bear no more. She pushed past Ruthie and Stirling and bolted through the swinging doors. She ran through the kitchen and past the stoves with huge, steaming kettles of soup. She burst out the back door into the alley. Once she was outside, her legs felt wobbly, and she sagged against the hard brick wall.

In a moment, Ruthie and Stirling were beside her. "Kit?" said Ruthie gently. "Are you okay?"

Kit nodded. "Is my dad still . . ." she began.

"Your dad left," said Ruthie. "He said he'd talk to you at home."

Kit took a shaky breath.

"Come on," said Ruthie. "Let's go." Stirling grabbed the wagon handle, and they started down the alley with the empty wagon rattling and banging noisily behind

them. Slowly, without talking, the three of them walked
together until they came to the end of Ruthie's driveway.
They stopped next to the stack of lumber left over from the
new garage, and Ruthie turned to Kit. "Listen," she said.
"Everything's going to be all right."

"All right?" Kit repeated. She shivered. "No, Ruthie,"
she said. "Everything's *not* going to be all right. My father
hasn't been having job interviews. He's been going to a
soup kitchen. He had to, just to get something to *eat*, to get
food for our *family* to eat." Kit's voice shook. "Dad's not
going to get a job here in Cincinnati. Maybe he would have
a better chance of finding one in Chicago. I guess . . ." Kit
faltered, then went on. "I guess now I hope that he *will* go."

"No, you don't," said Stirling in his husky voice.

Kit frowned. "What do *you* know about what I want?"
she asked. "*Your* father is in Chicago, sending you letters
with money stuck in them!"

"No," said Stirling. His gray eyes looked straight at Kit.
"He isn't."

"What are you talking about?" asked Kit. "I saw the
money!"

"That was *my* twenty dollars," Stirling said. "My father
gave it to me before he left. He told me to save it for an
emergency." Stirling sighed, and then he poured out the
whole story. "My mother hasn't been able to pay any rent

since we moved in," he said. "I offered her the twenty dollars lots of times, but she always said no. Then, a few weeks ago, she told me that we were going to have to leave your house. I knew it was because she was ashamed to stay any longer without paying. She wouldn't feel so bad if she could help with the housework, but your mother won't let her. I figured if I could trick her into taking the twenty dollars, she might use it for rent. So I made her think it came in a letter from my father."

Kit squinted at Stirling, trying to understand. "You sneaked the money into the letter?" she asked.

Stirling shook his head. "No," he said. "It's worse than that." He paused. "I wrote the letter myself. I typed it on your typewriter."

"*What?*" Kit and Ruthie asked together.

"The truth ..." Stirling hesitated. "The truth is, I don't know where my father is," he said. "But I'm pretty sure he's never coming back here to my mother and me. He flew the coop, as Roger said. So that's how I know that you don't want your dad to go away, Kit. No matter what, it's better to have your dad at home. No matter how bad or hopeless things are, you don't want him to leave."

Kit sat down hard in the wagon.

"Stirling," said Ruthie, "you'd better tell your mom what you did."

Stirling nodded. It was as if he'd used up all his words.

Ruthie waved good-bye and went inside her house.

Kit stood up tiredly. As she trudged home with the wagon and Stirling behind her, a new thought presented itself: *When Stirling tells his mother about the letter and the money, they'll leave. They won't live here in our house anymore.*

Of course, Kit had wanted Stirling and his fussbudgety mother to leave ever since they'd arrived. But now . . . it was very peculiar. Now that it was about to happen, Kit did not feel glad. She opened her front door and stood in the hall, which smelled of wet wool coats, and watched Stirling head upstairs to the room he and his mother shared.

"Is that you, lamby?" Mrs. Howard called. "Did you wipe your feet?"

Stirling looked back over his shoulder at Kit, and a quicksilvery smile slipped across his face. Then he turned away and climbed the rest of the stairs.

Slowly, Kit took off her coat and headed upstairs to change out of her school clothes. As she passed by Mother and Dad's room, the door opened.

"Kit," said Dad. "Come in here, please. I'd like to talk to you."

Kit went in and stood facing Dad.

"I've already told your mother about what happened today," said Dad. "I owed her an apology, and I owe you

and Charlie one, too. I'm sorry I misled all of you. I should have told you what I was really doing. I've been going to the soup kitchen for weeks now, to eat and to get food to bring home. It was the only way I could contribute to the household."

"Are we . . . are we really that poor?" Kit whispered.

"Yes," said Dad. "We are. But I didn't want any of you to know. That's why I pretended not to be hungry here at home. I'd have lunch at the soup kitchen, and then I could give my breakfast or dinner away to make our groceries stretch further." Dad put his hand on Kit's shoulder. "I shouldn't have led you to believe that I'd find a job here in Cincinnati. I guess my excuse is that I wanted it to be true.

"But," said Dad, "it's time for me—for all of us—to face the truth. And the truth is that there's no point in studying the want ads in the newspapers every day for a job that's never going to appear. So your mother and I have decided. I'm going to Chicago."

"Oh, Dad!" cried Kit. "You're not going to Chicago because of that letter from Stirling's father, are you? That letter—"

Dad held up his hand to stop her. "I'm going," he said, "because there's really no alternative. We don't have room in the house to take in as many boarders as we need. If I go to Chicago, maybe I can find a job and send money home."

"I don't want you to go, Dad," Kit said desperately.

"You'll have to write to me and tell me what happens after I leave," Dad said, smiling a small smile. "It'll be like the old days. Remember the newspapers you used to make for me? I loved them so much. When I'm gone, will you write newspapers and send them to me so I won't feel so far away?"

Kit nodded slowly.

"That's my girl," said Dad. "You were my reporter during the good times. I need you to be my reporter during the hard times, too."

*Hard times*, thought Kit dully as she left Dad and walked down the hallway. Kit heard Miss Hart and Miss Finney laughing in their room and Mr. Peck teaching Charlie to play his big double bass fiddle. Mother needed her to set the table for dinner and scrub the potatoes and put them in the oven to bake. Then there was laundry to iron and fold and put away, all before dinner. *This is it*, Kit thought. *This is the truth of my life now.*

With heavy, defeated steps, Kit climbed the stairs to the attic. How foolish she had been to think that her life

was going to go back to the way it used to be! Kit sank
into her desk chair. She had been wrong about so many
things! Instead of resenting the boarders, she should have
been grateful for them. Instead of wanting them to leave,
she should have been trying to figure out a way to fit more
boarders into the house. Because . . . Kit felt pinpricks of
fear up her spine. Because there was no guarantee that Dad
would be able to find a job in Chicago, either. What would
become of her family? How would they have enough
money for food and clothes and heat? Would they be so
poor they'd be kicked out of their house?

*Oh, I wish we had room for more boarders!* Kit thought
passionately. *Then Dad could stay.*

Kit felt a drop of water on her hand. She looked up and
saw a new leak in the roof, right above her desk. Drops of
water plopped onto the papers next to her. Kit saw that the
drops had blurred one of her tree house sketches. *Oh well,
what difference does it make?* she thought, shoving the papers
aside. *Dad won't be here to build it. There's no use for the sketch
or Ruthie's lumber now.* Kit sat bolt upright. *Unless . . . wait a
minute! Tree house? Boardinghouse?*

Suddenly, Kit had an idea.

As soon as Kit and Mother were alone in the kitchen,
washing the dishes after dinner, Kit said, "Mother, I've

been thinking. Ruthie's father has a stack of lumber left over from their new garage. He said Ruthie and I could have it to build a tree house. But I bet he wouldn't mind if we used the lumber to fix up Charlie's sleeping porch instead. If we made it nice enough, then maybe Mr. Peck would move in with Charlie."

"And then?" Mother asked.

"Then we could put two new boarders in Mr. Peck's room," said Kit.

"We could certainly use the money," said Mother. She sighed tiredly. "But I just don't know if I could handle the extra work that two more boarders would be." Her face looked sad. "Especially after your father leaves."

"How about asking Mrs. Howard to help you with the housework instead of paying rent?" asked Kit. "Mrs. Howard is a crackerjack cleaner."

Mother shook her head. "I'm not sure she'd agree to that," she said.

"Oh, I think she would," said Kit. "Stirling says she *wants* to help."

Mother was quiet for a thoughtful moment. Then she said, "Kit, dear, it's very ingenious of you to have thought of all this, and it would be very nice of you and Ruthie to sacrifice your tree house lumber. But I'm afraid lumber for the renovation is not our only problem. We don't have money to pay a carpenter. Who'd do the work?"

"Dad could do it!" said Kit. "He's great at building things."

"Yes," agreed Mother. "But the idea would have to be presented to him in just the right way. Now that he's decided to go, it'll be hard to change his mind."

Kit grinned from ear to ear. "You leave that to me," she said, full of enthusiasm. "I have a great plan!"

Mother smiled. "All right," she said. "Give it a try!"

"Thanks, Mother!" said Kit. She hugged Mother and then darted out the kitchen door and flew up the stairs two at a time. She couldn't carry out her plan alone, but she knew just whom to ask for help.

Kit knocked on Stirling's door.

"Yes?" said Mrs. Howard. When she opened the door, Kit saw that the room was as neat as a pin.

"May I please speak to Stirling?" asked Kit.

Mrs. Howard began to say no. "He's very tired, and—"

But then Stirling appeared from behind his mother.

"Stirling," said Kit, looking straight at him. "Will you help me?"

"Yes!" said Stirling immediately. It was as though he'd been waiting for Kit's question for a long time.

The next morning, when Dad sat down to breakfast, this is what he saw at his place:

# The Hard Times News
## SPECIAL THANKSGIVING DAY EDITION
✳✳✳✳✳✳✳✳✳✳✳✳✳✳✳✳✳✳✳✳✳✳✳✳✳✳✳✳✳✳✳✳✳✳✳

Editor: Kit Kittredge
Artist: Stirling Howard
Adviser: ~~Mother~~ Margaret Kittredge

\*WANTED\*

Tall bearded man to share sleeping
porch with early rising, agreeable
teenager. Must play ~~double~~ double bass and ~~and~~
drink coffee. Call Charlie Kittredge.

\*WANTED\*

Do you have interesting, ~~xexciting~~ stories
to tell about adventures in nursing? If so,
I'd like to hear them! Call ~~Kitk~~ Kittredge.

\*WANTED IMMEDIATELY\*

Talented handy man to fix sleeping porch
so ~~that~~ it will sleep two. Great ~~workingg~~
conditions! Call the Kittredge family.

\*WANTED\*

Neat and tidy lady to help with housekeeping in exchange for room and board.
Call Margaret Kittredge..

\*WANTED\*

Kids with wagon to haul away ~~and~~
leftover lumber suitable for use in fixing
sleeping porch. Call Ruthie Smithens.

Kit, Stirling, and Mother sat on the edges of their seats watching Dad read *The Hard Times News*. When he finished reading, Dad glanced at Mother over the top of the paper with a questioning look. Mother smiled and nodded, and then Dad smiled, too.

"Well!" said Dad, patting the paper. "Look at this! There's a construction job in these want ads. A boarding-house needs to expand. It's right here in Cincinnati, close to home." Dad winked at Kit. "In fact, it is at home. It's the perfect job for me!"

Kit ran to Dad and hugged him. "So you'll stay, then?" she asked.

"Yes," said Dad. "I'll go talk to Ruthie's father about the leftover lumber today." He handed Kit's newspaper to Mrs. Howard. "I think there's a job here that might interest you, Mrs. Howard," he said.

Mrs. Howard read the want ads and exclaimed, "My land! So there is!" She turned to Mother. "I'd love to help you with the housekeeping," she said. "I'm very good at dusting. I've noticed that the upstairs hallway—"

"That's Kit's job," Mother interrupted politely. "But with two more boarders moving in soon, there'll be plenty to do. I'll be glad to have your help."

"I'll start today!" said Mrs. Howard.

Kit stood next to Dad and looked around the breakfast

table as the newspaper was passed from hand to hand. Charlie and Mr. Peck were laughing and talking together about being roommates. Miss Hart and Miss Finney were beaming at Kit, looking as if they were brimming over with stories to tell. Suddenly, she heard a quiet voice next to her say, "Happy Thanksgiving, Kit."

It was Stirling. His gray eyes were shining. Kit smiled. "Happy Thanksgiving, Stirling," she said.

# Rickrack

A fter that, the Kittredges' house seemed more cheerful, more like the home that Kit remembered before Dad lost his job. It was still crowded with boarders, but now the boarders seemed like friends. Thanksgiving *was* a happy day, full of laughter and lively chatter.

But money was still tight. November turned into December, and Dad still hadn't found a job.

On a bright, brisk Saturday afternoon two weeks before Christmas, Kit and Ruthie were cheerfully skittering down the sidewalk together like blown leaves. They were going to the movies, which they loved to do. When the girls were close to the movie theater, Kit leaned forward. She put her fists in her pockets and pushed down so that the front of her coat covered more of her dress.

"Hey, Kit, are you okay?" asked Ruthie kindly. "Does your stomach hurt or something?"

"No," said Kit. "I'm fine."

"Then how come you're all hunched over like that?" asked Ruthie.

"I'm pushing my coat down," said Kit, "because I don't

want everyone to see the rickrack on my dress."

"Why not?" asked Ruthie. "It's cute."

"Cute?" said Kit. "I hate it! My mother
sewed it over the crease that was left when
she let the hem down. I think it looks
terrible!" Actually, Kit felt as if the rickrack

*rickrack*

were a big, embarrassing sign that said to everyone, *Look at
this old outgrown dress I have to wear because I'm too poor to get
a new one!* But she did not explain that to Ruthie.

Luckily, Ruthie was the kind of friend who was helpful
even without explanations. "Walk behind me," she said.
"I'll cover you up. Once we're inside the movie theater, it'll
be dark and no one will see."

"Okay," said Kit. She scooched up behind Ruthie, and
the girls went into the theater. It was very warm inside.
The air was buttery with the aroma of hot popcorn. And of
course Ruthie was right—it *was* dark. Even so, when Kit sat
down, she spread her coat over her lap to hide the rickrack.

"Want some?" asked Ruthie, generously offering her
popcorn to Kit.

"Thanks," said Kit. She took just two pieces of popcorn
so that Ruthie wouldn't think she was a moocher. She
already felt prickles of guilt because Ruthie had paid for
her movie ticket.

But as soon as the newsreel began, Kit was very glad

she had given in and accepted Ruthie's generosity. Because there on the screen was Kit's absolute heroine, Amelia Earhart—the first woman in history to fly a plane across the Atlantic Ocean all by herself. Kit stared at the movie screen as Amelia Earhart, in a sporty jacket, flight cap, and gloves, saluted the camera and climbed into the cockpit of her plane. Kit listened to the rumble of the plane's motor. She could almost feel the little plane straining to go faster, faster, faster as Amelia Earhart drove it down the runway. Then at last, she could feel the exhilaration of lifting up off the ground and soaring above the clouds!

*Amelia Earhart*

The newsreel ended and Kit sank back. She was so carried away by Amelia Earhart that the cartoon after the newsreel went by in a blur. When the feature movie began, Kit didn't even try to make sense of the story. It was about a silly woman in a tiara singing and dancing her way up a staircase shaped like a wedding cake.

At last the movie was over. Kit and Ruthie walked out into the late afternoon sunshine. Ruthie turned to Kit and said, "Wasn't she wonderful?"

"Yes!" Kit agreed with enthusiasm. "I loved watching her climb into that plane, and ..."

"Not Amelia Earhart," Ruthie laughed. "I meant Dottie Drew, the movie star!"

"Oh, *her*!" said Kit.

"Wasn't she beautiful?" breathed Ruthie. "Like a princess almost."

"Uh, sure," said Kit. She did not share Ruthie's fascination with movie stars and princesses, but she didn't want to be rude. Ruthie had paid for her ticket, after all. Kit might seem ungrateful if she said she thought the woman in the movie was silly.

But Ruthie knew Kit too well to be fooled. She grinned. "I bet you didn't notice Dottie Drew at all," she said. "I should have known you'd care more about Amelia Earhart. How come you're so crazy about her?"

"She's smart," said Kit. "She's brave, too. When she makes up her mind to do something, she doesn't let anything stop her. She flew her plane across the ocean all by herself! She didn't need help from anybody." Kit spoke with determination. "I want to be like her."

"I know just what you mean," said Ruthie. "It's the same with me." She sighed. "I love to imagine that I'm a movie star or a princess."

Kit didn't think her serious ambitions were the same as Ruthie's starry-eyed daydreams at all. "That's different, Ruthie," she said. "First of all, Amelia Earhart's a real person who does real things that really matter. Movie stars and princesses are only phony glitter and glamour. And

I don't imagine that I *am* Amelia Earhart. I want to be *like* her. Imagining that you're a princess is just make-believe."

"So?" Ruthie shrugged. "There's nothing wrong with make-believe."

"Maybe not," said Kit. "But imaginary stuff doesn't solve any problems or help anything."

"Oh, I think it does," said Ruthie. "Make-believe can take your mind off your troubles for a while. That's a help."

On the sidewalk ahead of the girls, Kit saw a sad sight. It was a pile of household goods dumped on the curb. A bed frame leaned against a chair, and a lamp lay sideways on the ground. Books, clothes, and pots and pans were jumbled together in a heap. "Look," Kit said to Ruthie, pointing to the pile. "That stuff belongs to a family that's been evicted.

They've been thrown out of their house because they can't pay for it anymore. You've got to admit that make-believe and imagination are not going to help *them*."

"They should've imagined a way to get money," Ruthie said. "They could've done *something*."

"I'm sure they tried," said Kit, thinking of how hard her own family struggled to pay the bills every month. "Maybe they just couldn't keep up."

"Then," said Ruthie, "they should have asked their friends for help."

"Maybe they were too proud to do that," said Kit.

Ruthie shook her head sadly. "And look where their pride got them—thrown out on the street," she said. "It won't be a very merry Christmas for their family, will it?"

"No," said Kit. "It won't." She shivered. "Come on," she said to Ruthie. "Let's run. It'll warm us up."

"Last one home is a rotten egg!" said Ruthie.

The girls ran the rest of the way to Kit's house. Kit quickly helped her mother scrub potatoes and put them in the oven before she and Ruthie went upstairs.

The girls were engaged in a secret project with Miss Hart and Miss Finney. The nurses had helped the girls unravel old sweaters and then use the wool to knit scarves. The scarves were almost finished, except for the fringe. Kit and Ruthie planned to give their scarves to their fathers for

Christmas. Miss Hart planned to give hers to her boyfriend. Miss Finney said she wasn't sure which lucky guy would get her scarf. She couldn't decide between Tarzan and Franklin Roosevelt, who had just been elected president.

"Any news from Miss Hart's boyfriend lately?" asked Ruthie as the girls walked down the hall.

"Yup," said Kit. "He's coming to Cincinnati at Christmastime."

Long letters in fat envelopes still arrived nearly every day from Miss Hart's boyfriend in Boston. Miss Hart wrote back just as often, and her letters were just as long. Kit and Ruthie were curious about the letters, and Ruthie especially liked to keep an eye on the progress of Miss Hart's romance.

"Miss Hart must be thrilled," said Ruthie. "Oh, if only they could have a romantic date while he's here! He'd probably ask her to marry him!"

"Miss Hart's boyfriend is a student in medical school," said Kit. "It'll take all his money to travel here. I don't think he'll have any left over for a fancy date."

"I wish he would," said Ruthie dreamily. "Miss Finney and Mr. Peck could go, too, and *they'd* fall in love. That's what would happen if they were in a movie."

"Well," said Kit crisply. "They're not in a movie. They're in real life."

"Too bad," sighed Ruthie.

Kit knocked on the door to Miss Hart and Miss Finney's room. There was no answer. "I guess they're working the weekend shift at the hospital," Kit said. "We won't be able to finish our scarves today. Want to go up to my room and make a newspaper instead?"

"Sure!" said Ruthie with enthusiasm.

"We'll write about Amelia Earhart," said Kit.

"And Dottie Drew!" insisted Ruthie.

"Okay," said Kit, grinning. "Her, too." And she danced up the attic stairs to her room the way Dottie Drew had danced up the wedding cake in the movie.

Ruthie leaned over Kit's shoulder. Kit was typing a paragraph Ruthie had written about Dottie Drew. "Wait a minute," Ruthie said. "It's Dottie Drew, not Duttio Drow. And she's a movie star, not a muvio tar. You better fix those mistakes."

"I can't," sighed Kit. "My typewriter keys are broken. The *o* looks like a *u* and the *e* looks like an *o*. And the *s* doesn't work at all anymore."

"Oh, well, that's okay," said Ruthie. She grinned, and then said slowly, "I mean . . . uh, woll. That ukay."

Kit grinned, too. "I guess people will figure it out," she said. "Anyway, the pictures are great."

The girls had had the smart idea of asking Stirling

to draw sketches of Amelia Earhart and Dottie Drew to illustrate their newspaper. "Stirling's a good artist," said Ruthie as she looked through his sketchpad. "See how he made Amelia Earhart look like you, Kit, freckles and all?"

Kit nodded. "And he put *you* in Dottie Drew's fancy ball gown and tiara," she said.

"That's me. Princess Ruthie," giggled Ruthie, striking a princessly pose.

Kit looked at the paper in her typewriter. "There's still a little space left," she said. "What should we write about?"

"Christmas!" said Ruthie. "We can say, 'Christmas is coming!' Everyone loves to read about that. I love everything about Christmas. What's your most favorite part, Kit?"

"Christmas Eve," said Kit. "That's when we put up our tree. Charlie's going to get us a free tree this year. We always decorate our tree on Christmas Eve. It looks so beautiful, especially the lights. We turn them on when we finish decorating, and we have dinner next to the tree. Mother always makes waffles. It's our tradition. I love it."

"I love the tradition that you and I have," said Ruthie, "when we go downtown with our mothers on the day after Christmas."

"Ruthie," Kit began, "I'm sorry. I'm afraid—"

But Ruthie talked over her. "I know you and your

mother are awfully busy this year, what with the boarding-house and all," she said. "So I was thinking that maybe this Christmas, instead of the whole day, we could go downtown just for a few hours. That'd be just as fun, wouldn't it?"

Kit believed in telling the truth, even when it was hard. "Time isn't the only problem, Ruthie," she said. "My mother and I don't have any money for lunch at a fancy restaurant or tickets to a show. We don't have money for presents even. Not this year."

"That's what I figured," said Ruthie. "So I thought we could change our tradition and just go window-shopping and have a winter picnic or something."

"I think," said Kit slowly, "it would wreck our tradition to change it."

"We wouldn't change *all* of it," said Ruthie. "We'd still get all dressed up in our best dresses, and—"

"I'd have to wear this rickrack dress," Kit cut in, "which I hate." She knew she sounded like a sourpuss, but she couldn't help it.

"But it's *Christmas*," Ruthie insisted. "You never know what might happen. You might get a new dress."

Kit shook her head. "The last thing I want my family to do this Christmas is to spend money on me," she said. "I don't want dresses or outings or presents. The only thing I want is to find a way to make money."

"Find a wicked ogre," said Ruthie. "Lots of times in fairy tales a princess is kind to an ogre, and then he spins straw into gold for her, or he enchants her so that jewels come out of her mouth when she talks, or he grants her three wishes."

Kit felt annoyed at Ruthie and her princesses. She and her family were real people, not characters in a fairy tale. "For Pete's sake!" she said. "It takes work, not wishes, to solve problems. That make-believe stuff is silly. There are no ogres in Cincinnati."

Ruthie just grinned. "Watch out," she said. "If you're not nice, the ogre'll make snakes and toads come out of your mouth. How'd you like that?"

"Not much," said Kit. Impatiently, she pushed the silver arm that moved the paper up and out of the typewriter. But she pushed a little too hard, because, to her horror, the silver arm came off in her hand. "Oh no!" she cried, holding it up for Ruthie to see. "Look what I've done! Oh, now the typewriter won't work at all!"

"Come on," said Ruthie, heading for the stairs. "Let's go get your dad. I bet he can fix it."

"I sure hope so," said Kit.

The two girls hurried downstairs. They paused in the hallway outside the living room because they heard Kit's parents talking to someone. The conversation sounded serious, so they knew they shouldn't barge in and interrupt.

Kit's dad was talking. "The room should be ready by the middle of January," he said. "Then we can take in two more boarders."

"I'm afraid that'll be too late," said the other voice.

The girls looked at each other in surprise. It was Ruthie's dad, Mr. Smithens, speaking. Ruthie started to go into the room, but Kit held her back.

"I've come today as a friend," said Mr. Smithens. "Your name is on a list of people who owe money to the bank, people who are behind on their mortgage payments. I came to warn you that if you can't catch up on your payments, the bank will take your house and you'll be evicted."

*Evicted!* Kit felt as if she'd been punched in the stomach.

"I'll hold off the bank until after the holidays," Ruthie's dad said. "But if you can borrow the money from some-one, you should. Do you think your aunt in Kentucky might help, Jack? Or, Margaret, how about your uncle here in Cincinnati?"

Kit's mother started to answer, saying, "Well, I—"

"Thanks, Stan," Kit's dad interrupted. "We'll figure something out."

Kit could hardly breathe. Evicted! She and her family were going to be thrown out of their house! All of their belongings would be tossed out onto the sidewalk, just like those she and Ruthie had seen on their way home from the movies. *It's going to happen to my family,* she thought. *It's going to happen to me.* She shuddered, and Ruthie touched her arm.

"Oh, Kit," Ruthie whispered, "What'll you do? I wish . . ."

*Wish!* thought Kit. She jerked her arm away. She couldn't bear to hear Ruthie say one of her silly things about wishes and princesses and make-believe. Not now. It was bad enough that Ruthie had been there to overhear the terrible, humiliating news! Without a word, Kit turned sharply and went back up the stairs to her room, leaving Ruthie all alone in the hall.

# The Bright
# Red Dress

## CHAPTER 10

**T**hat night, after the last dinner dish was washed and dried, Mother took off her apron, put on her hat and coat, and went out. She didn't say where she was going, but Kit knew. Mother was paying a visit to Uncle Hendrick, who lived alone in a big, gloomy house near downtown Cincinnati. Kit knew Mother was going to ask Uncle Hendrick for money so that they wouldn't be evicted.

Kit was reading in bed when Mother returned. When she came up to kiss Kit good night, Kit could see that her mother's face was tired.

"Uncle Hendrick said no, didn't he?" said Kit.

Mother was surprised. "How did—" she began.

"I heard Mr. Smithens talking to you and Dad," Kit said in her straightforward way. "I know about us being evicted. I figured you went to Uncle Hendrick to ask for money. And," Kit repeated, "he said no, didn't he?"

"I'm sorry, Kit," Mother said sadly. "It's not fair for a child to have to worry about such things." She sighed. "But you're right. Uncle Hendrick believes that money must be earned by hard work, not given away. He says if we are evicted, he wants us to move in with him."

Kit sat bolt upright. "Oh, no!" she said. "We'd hate that! All the boarders would leave. It'd be awful."

Mother smiled a sad smile. "We may not have a choice," she said. "And we may lose the boarders anyway. At this point, we don't have enough money to pay even the electric bill. We can't ask the boarders to stay if our electricity is cut off and we don't have any lights."

Kit couldn't bear to see Mother look so defeated. "I'll help," she said. "I promise. I'll find a way to make money."

"Well," said Mother, "there is a way you can help, though I don't think it'll make any money. Uncle Hendrick says he's ill. I think he's really just lonely and fretful. But he wants me to come back tomorrow and every day until he feels better. I'm so busy here, I don't see how I can. Would you do it? You'd start tomorrow, and next week you could go after school. During Christmas vacation, you could stay for a few hours every day. He needs someone to keep him company and do errands and walk his dog."

Kit's heart sank. Uncle Hendrick's old black Scottie dog, Inky, was the meanest, most hateful dog in Cincinnati. He was even meaner than Uncle Hendrick. And Uncle Hendrick was exactly like mean, miserly Ebenezer Scrooge in *A Christmas Carol* before the ghosts visited him and scared him into being nice.

"I know it's a lot to ask," said Mother. "But it would be a great help to me."

"I'll do it," said Kit. This was her chance to help.

Mother hugged Kit. "That's my girl," she said, and now her smile was real. "Thank you. Uncle Hendrick knows we don't have a car anymore. He gave me a nickel for the streetcar. I'll give it to you tomorrow. Now don't read too long. You need to rest. Good night!"

"Good night!" said Kit.

The first bad thing that happened when Kit set forth to visit Uncle Hendrick was that she missed the streetcar. She had to run all the way to Uncle Hendrick's house because she was supposed to be there promptly at noon and Uncle Hendrick was a stickler for time. Luckily, Kit was a fast runner. But it was very cold, and Kit's nose was red and her hair was blown every which way by the time she got to Uncle Hendrick's door. She tried to catch her breath and straighten herself up a little. But Inky was barking wildly and scrabbling his claws against the other side of the door, so Uncle Hendrick opened it before she even knocked. That was the next bad thing.

"What are *you* doing here?" he bellowed over Inky's yapping.

"Mother's too busy," Kit bellowed back. "I'm here instead."

"What are **you** doing here?" Uncle Hendrick bellowed over Inky's yapping.

"I don't want *you*," said Uncle Hendrick. "Go away!"

Inky growled as if to echo Uncle Hendrick, and then launched into another frenzy of barking.

Kit didn't budge. She'd promised Mother that she would help. It would take more than Uncle Hendrick's bluster and Inky's snarls to discourage her.

"Well, you're here, so you might as well stay," said Uncle Hendrick. "Hurry up! Don't stand there like a fool and let the heat out. It costs good money." Kit stepped inside, and he shut the door behind her, saying, "Come with me."

"Yes, sir," said Kit. Now that the door was shut, she realized how dark it was inside Uncle Hendrick's house. The darkness seemed old somehow, and permanent, as if it had been there a long time and always would be there. Kit followed Uncle Hendrick and Inky upstairs to Uncle Hendrick's huge room. He sat down in the most comfortable chair by the coal fire and put a blanket over his knees. Inky jumped up into the other chair by the fire. He watched Kit's every move with his sharp, unfriendly black eyes.

Kit went to Uncle Hendrick to give him the nickel she hadn't used. "This is the nickel you gave Mother for the streetcar," said Kit. "I missed the streetcar, so I—"

"I don't care if you came on a winged chariot," Uncle Hendrick said, impatiently pushing her hand away. "You got here on time. That's all that matters."

"You mean I can keep the nickel?" asked Kit.

"Yes!" barked Uncle Hendrick, sounding a lot like Inky. "Now stop jabbering! Hand me my book! Not the red one, the brown one! And how am I supposed to read it? Hand me my eyeglasses, too, and be quick about it."

It seemed to Kit that for an old man who was supposed to be sick, Uncle Hendrick certainly had plenty of energy for bossing her around and pointing out what she was doing wrong, which was everything. She filled his teacup too full and sloshed tea into the saucer. She wobbled the spoon when she poured his medicine into it. She pulled too hard on the cord that closed the drapes but didn't push hard enough when moving his chair. She talked too fast and walked too slow. There was no pleasing Uncle Hendrick.

Inky was just as bad. When it was time for his walk, Kit put her coat on. She clipped Inky's leash onto his collar. "Come, Inky," she said. Inky didn't move.

"You'll have to carry him," said Uncle Hendrick. "He doesn't like walking down the stairs."

Kit hoisted the fat old dog up in her arms and carried him down the stairs and out the door. Once his feet hit the sidewalk, Inky took off. He strained on the leash, practically pulling Kit's arm out of its socket. When they got to the park, Inky sat down on the grass and refused to move. Kit had to drag Inky back to Uncle Hendrick's house and carry him upstairs.

"You," Kit hissed as she set him down, "are a horrible dog."

Inky's black eyes glittered. He looked pleased with himself. He jumped into his chair and promptly went to sleep.

Uncle Hendrick was asleep, too. So Kit had to sit perfectly still and wait for him to wake up. She amused herself by thinking of words to describe Uncle Hendrick and Inky. *They're both grouchy and grumpy*, she thought. *They're crabby, cranky, critical, and cross.*

When at last Uncle Hendrick woke up, he announced that it was time for Kit to go home. Kit put on her coat, which was now covered with Inky's black hair.

"Good-bye," she said to Uncle Hendrick. "I'll see you tomorrow."

"Humph," said Uncle Hendrick. He didn't sound pleased or displeased. He reached into his pocket and pulled out two nickels. "Here," he said. "One for the streetcar home and one for the streetcar here tomorrow. Take them and go!" So Kit did.

When she closed the door behind her, Kit took a deep

breath. The cold, clean winter air felt wonderful on her cheeks. It cleared the stuffy, mediciney, doggy smell of Uncle Hendrick's house out of her nose. As Kit walked to the streetcar stop, she had an idea.

*I'll walk home*, she thought. *Uncle Hendrick said he didn't care if I use the nickels for the streetcar or not. I won't use them. I'll save them and give them to Mother to help pay the electric bill. That will be my Christmas surprise for her.*

The thought cheered Kit, and she turned up her collar and started the long walk home with determined steps. But it was awfully cold, and the walk was all uphill. By the time Kit got to her house, she was tired and cold to the bone. She was hungry, too. It was disheartening to know she had missed Sunday dinner and there'd be only crackers and milk for supper.

When Kit opened the front door, she was surprised to see Ruthie sitting on the bottom step in the front hall. Ruthie had a big white box on her lap. Her face was bright and eager. She looked as if she was struggling to hold a surprise inside and was about to burst. "Hi!" she said to Kit. "I thought you'd never get here!" She jumped up from the stair and thrust the big white box at Kit. "Here!" she said. "This is for you." Ruthie was so excited, she danced around Kit impatiently as Kit knelt down to open the box. "Wait till you see!" she said. "Now everything will be okay!"

Kit lifted the lid of the box. Inside was a bright red dress. She took it out, puzzled. "But this is your dress, Ruthie," she said at last.

"It *was*," said Ruthie. "It's my last year's Christmas dress. It doesn't fit me anymore. I'm getting a new one, so I'm giving this one to you."

The bright red dress was *so* red it seemed to make Kit's hands warm just to hold it. Kit felt her face get warm, too, but the heat came from the burning sting of embarrassment. She was humiliated, not delighted, by Ruthie's hand-me-down present. *Now Ruthie thinks of me as a poor, pitiful beggar girl*, she thought. Kit swallowed. "Thanks," she managed to say politely. She tried very hard to smile.

"That's not all!" Ruthie burbled. "Look in the pocket!"

Kit reached into the pocket of the dress and pulled out four tickets to the ballet. There was also an invitation in Ruthie's handwriting that said:

> Mrs. Smithens and Ruthie Smithens
> cordially invite
> Mrs. Kittredge and Kit Kittredge
> to a fancy tea at
> Shillito's Restaurant
> on December 26th
> after the ballet

"See?" said Ruthie, all aglow. "My mother bought the tickets, and she'll pay for the tea. Now we *can* have our special day. And you won't have to wear your rickrack dress."

Slowly, Kit slid the invitation and the tickets back into the pocket. She folded the dress carefully and put the lid back on the box. She stood up. "Thank you, Ruthie," she said stiffly. "But your dress is probably too big for me. And my mother and I are going to be busy on December twenty-sixth." She handed the big white box to Ruthie.

Ruthie looked at the box and then at Kit. "What do you mean?" she asked.

"I have a job now," said Kit. "At my Uncle Hendrick's house."

"But you could take a day off," said Ruthie. "You could—"

"No," interrupted Kit coolly. "I couldn't. It's my responsibility." Ruthie's face looked so sad that Kit softened a bit. "Listen," she said. "I know you're just trying to be nice and generous, Ruthie. But don't you see? I can't wear your old dress."

"But my mother fixed it to fit you," said Ruthie. "And I thought you were embarrassed by the rickrack dress. I thought you hated it."

"I do hate it," said Kit. "But at least it's my own. I'd be embarrassed to wear your dress. And it's the same with the tickets and the tea. It would make my mother and me feel like sponges. We'd be ashamed to let your mother pay for us."

"Ashamed!" said Ruthie, pink in the face and mad. "I think you should be ashamed of being so selfish. You're only thinking of yourself! What about me? Did you ever stop to think that maybe you're ruining my Christmas with your stupid pride? You've got a houseful of people, and I'm all alone with just my mother and father. The most fun I ever have is with you. The day you and I spend together after Christmas is the very best part of Christmas for me. I thought you liked it, too. That's why my mother and I tried to fix it this year. But you're too stuck-up and stubborn to accept it. We were just trying to help."

"I don't want help," said Kit, bristling.

"Oh, I know!" said Ruthie. "You think you're just like great old Amelia Earhart, flying all by herself without help from anybody."

Now Kit was mad, too. "At least I'm not so babyish that I think I'm a princess like you do," she said. "You're always talking about wishes and wicked ogres and make-believe. You don't know anything that's real. Your father still has his job. You can do whatever you want. You have everything, except you don't have any idea what the world is really like!"

"Well, now I know what *you* are really like," said Ruthie. "Mean."

"Well, you're spoiled," said Kit.

"Oh!" exclaimed Ruthie angrily. She grabbed her coat and went to the door. "I don't think we can be friends anymore."

"Good!" said Kit.

"Good-*bye*!" said Ruthie. Then she left, closing the door firmly behind her.

Kit stared at the door for a second, and then turned and ran as fast as she could up the stairs to her room. She flung herself facedown on her bed. Oh, oh, *oh*! How could everything be so horrible? It wasn't *fair*. Her family had lost so much since Dad had lost his job. Not just money. They'd lost their feeling of being safe, their trust that things would work out for the best. They were probably going to lose their home. *And now I've lost the most important thing of all*, thought Kit. *My best friend.*

Kit buried her face in her pillow and cried.

# The Wicked Ogre

## CHAPTER 11

**K**it couldn't allow herself to cry for long. She knew that all her afternoon chores were waiting for her. And Mother liked to give the kitchen floor a good scrub every Sunday night because there wasn't time during the week. Kit rolled over and sat up on her bed. She saw Amelia Earhart smiling at her from the newspaper photograph near her desk. *Come on, Kit,* Amelia seemed to say. *Gotta get up and go.* Even though she still felt miserable, Kit wiped her eyes, blew her nose, and went downstairs to the kitchen.

Mother had already put the chairs up on the kitchen table. She was filling a bucket with hot, soapy water at the sink. She turned to greet Kit with a smile. But her smile faded when she saw Kit's eyes, red from crying. "Oh, Kit, darling!" she said. She dried her hands on her apron as she hurried over to put her arm around Kit. "Was it that bad at Uncle Hendrick's, then? He's so fussy. And that awful what's-his-name, too. The Scottie dog!"

"Inky," Kit said. Mother smelled of soapsuds, and Kit let herself lean against her. "He hates me."

"That's not all that's wrong, is it?" asked Mother.

"No," admitted Kit. "Ruthie and I had a fight." Kit poured out the whole story about Ruthie's bright red dress, the ballet tickets, and the invitation to tea. "It was wrong of me to say no for you, too, Mother," she said. "But I couldn't help it. I was just so *mad*." Kit sighed. "It used to be easy to be friends with Ruthie. It isn't anymore."

Mother nodded. "Your lives are very different now," she said. "Things that are possible for Ruthie are not possible for you."

"The truth is," said Kit, "I'm jealous of her."

"And she," said Mother, "is jealous of you."

"Of me?" asked Kit, surprised. "But I'm the one who's lost everything. Why would she be jealous of me?"

"Oh, I don't know," said Mother. "I've had the impression that Ruthie envies you for having the boarders around, like a big, interesting family. It's awfully quiet at her house. And maybe she envies how your life is more grown-up now. People trust you to do important things."

"I never thought of it that way," said Kit, sighing. "All I know is that I'm sorry about the fight."

"I wish we could use the telephone," said Mother. The telephone had been turned off because they could no longer afford to pay the bill. "Then you could call Ruthie and tell her that you're sorry. Well, you'll see her in school tomorrow. You can make it better then."

"Do you think so?" asked Kit hopefully.

"Of course!" said Mother. "It is never too late to repair a friendship." Mother lifted the pail of hot water out of the sink. "Let's scrub this floor now," she said. "I'm afraid it's never too late for that, either!"

Mother was wrong. Kit was not able to patch things up with Ruthie the next day. Ruthie didn't stop to pick her up before school. And every time Kit tried to get Ruthie's attention during the morning, Ruthie turned away or hid herself in a group of girls. At lunchtime, in desperation, Kit wrote Ruthie a note and put it on her desk. She watched unhappily as Ruthie glanced at it, picked it up in two fingers as if it were a dead toad, and tossed it, unopened and unread, into the wastepaper basket. Then Ruthie sashayed off to lunch with a bunch of girls who were in her dance class. Kit used to be in the class, too, but she'd had to drop out when her family couldn't afford *that* anymore, either.

Everyone at school noticed that Ruthie was shunning Kit. Stirling tried to help. "Here," he said to Kit. "Give this to Ruthie." He handed Kit a picture he had drawn on a sketchpad. The picture showed Kit flying an airplane like Amelia Earhart's. The passenger in the airplane was Ruthie dressed as a princess.

"Thanks, Stirling," Kit said. But she was afraid to give the drawing to Ruthie after what she'd said about princesses being babyish. So Kit put Stirling's sketchpad and drawing into her book bag.

After three days of getting the cold shoulder, Kit gave up. It was clear that Ruthie was too mad to forgive her. She wouldn't even give Kit a chance to apologize. When Ruthie had said they couldn't be friends anymore, she'd meant it. School closed for vacation, and Kit and Ruthie still hadn't spoken.

Usually, Kit loved Christmas vacation because it meant she had more time to spend with her family and Ruthie. But this year, all it meant was that she had more time to spend with Uncle Hendrick and Inky. Every morning, after doing her chores at home, Kit went to his house. She walked there and back so she could save the streetcar fare. Her pile of nickels was growing. But that was the only good thing about going to Uncle Hendrick's house.

"Good gracious, you careless child! Don't use so much string!" Uncle Hendrick fussed at her one day as Kit was tying up a bundle of newspapers for him. "Do you think string grows on trees? I suppose you learned your wasteful ways from your spendthrift parents." He snorted. "They think that money grows on trees. Holes in their pockets, those two!"

Kit bit her lip to stop herself from saying to Uncle Hendrick, "That's not true!" He never missed a chance to be critical of her parents. He lectured her about how they deserved their poverty because they'd been extravagant and lived beyond their means. It made Kit furious. Sometimes she thought Uncle Hendrick was trying to make her mad on purpose so that she wouldn't come back. But Kit could be ornery, too. The meaner Uncle Hendrick was, the more determined she was not to give up. She wouldn't give him that satisfaction.

At the end of every day, Uncle Hendrick had errands for her to do on her way home. Every errand came with lots of fussbudgety instructions. "Take these shoes to be shined," Uncle Hendrick commanded one blustery day. "Here's a dime to pay for it." He shook his finger at Kit. "Tell the man that I demand good value for my money. The last time, he left a scuff mark on the toe. Tell him don't think I didn't see it."

"Yes, sir," said Kit. She put the shoes in her book bag and the dime in her pocket.

"Leave these shirts at the laundry," Uncle Hendrick said. "Tell them to put starch on the collars and cuffs *only*. And tell them that I don't want to see any buttons broken like the last time or I'll deduct the cost of the buttons from their bill."

"Yes, sir," said Kit again. "Good-bye." She gathered up the shirts, put on her coat, and left.

The laundry was closest, so Kit dropped off the shirts first. Then she trudged along to the shoe-shine shop. When she got there, a terrible sight met her eyes. There was a big hand-lettered sign on the door:

**OUT OF BUSINESS**
*Closed till the Depression is Out of Business, too!*

Kit stood there in the bitter cold wondering what to do. One thing was sure. Uncle Hendrick would bite her head off and howl worse than Inky if she brought his shoes back unshined. So Kit took the shoes home. Using her dad's rags and polish, she shined them herself, rubbing until her arm ached. She carried the shoes back to Uncle Hendrick's house the next day, bracing herself for his persnickety words of criticism.

Before she could explain, Uncle Hendrick took the shoes from her. "There!" he said. "That's what I call a job well-done! Let that be a lesson to you, Kit. You only get your money's worth if you insist upon it."

Kit hid a smile. "Here's your dime back," she told him. "The shop was closed. I shined the shoes myself."

"You?" said Uncle Hendrick. He studied the shoes again, then narrowed his eyes at her. "Then you earned the dime," he said brusquely. "Keep it."

Kit put the dime in her pocket. Then she faced Uncle Hendrick bravely. "Uncle Hendrick," she said. "I've been thinking. May I work for you? If I pick up your groceries, may I keep the tip you usually give the deliveryman? If I deliver your letters, may I keep the cost of the stamps? And if I—"

"Stop!" shouted Uncle Hendrick. "You pester the life out of me! Get this straight once and for all, child. I don't care who does the work, as long as it's done to my satisfaction. You may keep any money you earn. Understand?"

"Yes, sir!" said Kit.

"Good!" said Uncle Hendrick. "Now don't bother me about this again."

That was all Kit needed to hear.

Starting then, whenever she could, Kit did Uncle Hendrick's jobs herself. She polished his shoes. She delivered his letters. She fetched his groceries. She brought him his newspaper. She washed his windows—and then washed them all over again because Uncle Hendrick said he saw streaks. Kit wanted to earn enough money to pay the electric bill, which she knew was about two dollars and thirty-five cents. Every day, she counted up the money she'd earned to see how close she was getting to her goal. Five days before Christmas Eve, Kit had one dollar and fifty-five cents. She needed eighty cents more. She knew she could earn ten cents a day by walking instead of riding the streetcar. That would be fifty cents. But it was going to be tough to earn the last thirty cents.

Still, Kit was determined, even though Uncle Hendrick's chores were hard. The winter streets were often slippery, and the winter darkness came earlier and earlier. But Kit kept saying to herself, *Think how surprised Mother will be when I give her the money I've earned.*

The thought kept her going when the cold wind made her eyes water and slush seeped through her shoes and froze her feet. Sometimes Kit had to take dreadful old Inky with her when she did errands. He'd wind his leash around her legs and try to trip her, or he'd roll in a puddle and then shake so that cold, dirty water splattered all over her. The *clink* of coins in her pocket helped Kit put up with Inky, and with Uncle Hendrick, too, even when he was at his most cantankerous.

There was one errand Kit liked to do even though it didn't earn her any money. Every few days, Uncle Hendrick sent her to the public library to return his books and pick up new ones the librarian set aside for him. The huge public library seemed like a hushed, warm heaven to Kit, filled as it was from floor to ceiling with books. Unfortunately, she never had time to linger there. Uncle Hendrick was always in a hurry to get his books, which seemed odd because they were so dull and boring they always put him to sleep.

It was during the afternoons while Uncle Hendrick dozed that Kit thought about Ruthie the most. She missed Ruthie. It would have been such a comfort to talk to her. She'd understand how hateful Inky was and how impossible Uncle Hendrick was.

One especially long afternoon, Kit sat watching Uncle Hendrick snore in his chair. One of his dull books had put him to sleep. Inky was contentedly snoring, too. Kit reached into her book bag only to find that she'd left the book she wanted to read at home. Instead, she pulled out a pad of paper. It was Stirling's sketchpad, the one he'd used when he made sketches of Kit as Amelia Earhart and Ruthie as a princess. Kit looked at the sketches. Then, without planning to, she began to write.

*Once upon a time,* she began. And then the story seemed to sweep her away. It wasn't the kind of story she usually wrote for her newspaper. This story was not about facts. It didn't report what was really happening. This story was about a completely different world, the kind of world Ruthie liked, a world that was imaginary. In this world,

Kit could make anything she
wanted to happen *happen*.

While she was writing,
Kit forgot she was stuck in
Uncle Hendrick's dreary
house. She forgot about her
family's money troubles, and
the fact that the boarders might
leave, and that her family might be
evicted from their house. All of that disappeared while she
was in the world of her story.

When Uncle Hendrick woke up and blinked his eyes
open, Kit felt herself snap back into the real world. It was
as if she were waking up, too, from a wonderful dream.
Kit hurriedly shoved the sketchpad back into her book
bag, thinking, *Ruthie was right! Make-believe does make your
troubles disappear for a while.* Kit wished she could tell Ruthie
that she understood about make-believe now. Then Kit
remembered that she and Ruthie weren't friends anymore.
They weren't even speaking to each other.

❧

After that first afternoon, Kit wrote more of her story
every day. She began to look forward to her writing time,
when the only sounds in the grim old house were Uncle
Hendrick's snores, the hollow ticking of the clock on the

mantel, and Inky's slobbery snuffles.

Soon Kit began to see that writing made *all* of her day better. She thought about her story when she was outside doing errands, and it distracted her from the cold and her tired feet. She paid close attention to how things looked or smelled or sounded, trying to find just the right words to describe them for her story.

When Uncle Hendrick woke up and fussed at her, it didn't bother her anymore. She listened carefully in case she wanted to use something he said in her story. Because Kit had discovered that Ruthie had been right about something else, too. There *was* a wicked ogre in Cincinnati: Uncle Hendrick.

# Jewels

## CHAPTER 12

**W**hooosh! A harsh wind blew sleet into Kit's face. She hunched her shoulders and wrapped her arms tightly around Uncle Hendrick's library books to keep them dry. It was Christmas Eve morning, and even a long list of errands and nasty weather could not dampen Kit's spirits. *I bet this sleet will turn into snow,* she thought. *How perfect! It'll be so cozy to have dinner next to the Christmas tree.*

Kit's family had not had time to put up their Christmas tree yet, so as soon as she was finished at Uncle Hendrick's this afternoon, she'd hurry home and help Dad and Charlie put up the tree and decorate it. Kit skipped with happiness, thinking of how surprised everyone would be when she gave Mother the money she had earned. Two dollars and forty cents—enough to pay the electric bill! She had earned the last thirty-five cents by selling Uncle Hendrick's rags to the ragman. *Now the boarders won't leave,* she thought. *Now we can light the Christmas tree lights and our tree will be as beautiful as every other year.*

Kit let herself into Uncle Hendrick's house. Inky barked at her as she climbed the stairs and nipped at her feet as she went into Uncle Hendrick's room. "Stop that, Inky," said Kit. But Inky was restless, prowling from window to window. Whenever the sleet clattered against the glass, sounding like a handful of thrown pebbles, Inky barked. Every once in a while, there'd be a loud *CRACK!* when a tree limb, weighed down by a heavy coating of ice, would snap. Inky howled whenever that happened.

When it was time for Inky's walk after lunch, the dog stubbornly refused to go out, so Kit had to carry him, squirming and yowling, out the back door. "Go ahead and yowl," she said to him. "Even you can't ruin this day for me, you horrible dog." She shivered as she waited for Inky to come back inside. It was bitterly cold, and the sleet showed no signs of stopping. Kit tilted her head to look at the sky. It looked gray and hard, as if it, too, were encased in ice.

At last it was time for Kit to go home. She quickly put on her coat and grabbed her book bag. She knew it was going to be a difficult and slippery walk home, and she was anxious to get started. "Good-bye," she said to Uncle Hendrick. "We'll see you tomorrow." Uncle Hendrick was feeling much better, so he planned to take a cab to the Kittredges' house for Christmas Day.

"What? Oh! Yes, of course," said Uncle Hendrick. "Go along now. And close the door carefully behind you. I don't want it banging in this wind."

"Yes, sir!" said Kit. Joyfully, she pounded down the stairs and opened the door. A cruel blast of wind pushed so hard against her that she stumbled back. She bent her head forward, burying her chin in her collar. Ice slashed at her cheeks and stung her eyes. The streetlights were lit, and the tree branches were shiny with ice and glittered as if they were made of diamonds.

Kit took a step forward, and her feet flew out from under her. She landed hard on her bottom, so hard that she saw stars. Gingerly, Kit rolled to her hands and knees and tried to stand. She clutched at the iron railing that fenced Uncle Hendrick's yard and inched her way to the sidewalk. It was slow going, and when the iron railing ended and there was nothing to hold on to, Kit fell again. This time she cracked her elbow so badly she winced with pain. Kit blinked back tears. She struggled to her feet again and tried to skate forward. But it was no use. For every step forward, she seemed to slip backward twice as far. If she couldn't make any headway on the flat ground, there was no way she could get up the steep hill home, or even to the streetcar stop. Kit's coat was beaded with pearls of ice, and her feet were so numb they were heavy as lead. Sadly, Kit fought her way back to Uncle Hendrick's house.

"What are you doing here?" Uncle Hendrick snapped when he saw her.

"It's too slippery out," said Kit. "May I wait here till the sleet stops?"

Uncle Hendrick peered out the window. "It's not going to stop tonight," he announced, sounding pleased to give such bad news. "You'll have to stay the night."

"Oh *no!*" wailed Kit. "I can't. It's Christmas Eve. I *have* to get home."

"Don't be ridiculous!" barked Uncle Hendrick. "Stop whining! There's nothing to be done. You'll have to call your family and tell them you're staying here tonight."

"I can't," said Kit.

"Why not?" asked Uncle Hendrick impatiently.

"Our phone's not connected anymore," said Kit.

"Couldn't pay the bill, I suppose," said Uncle Hendrick sourly. "Typical! Well, then you'll have to call someone who can go to your house to tell your parents where you are. Call a neighbor or a friend."

A friend? Now Kit's heart felt as heavy and leaden as her feet. There was only one person she could call, and that was the last person on earth she wanted to call. But Kit had no choice. She went to the phone.

*Maybe her mother will answer,* she thought. But when the voice on the other end of the line said hello, Kit knew who it was right away. "Ruthie?" she said.

"It's me." Kit spoke all in a rush. "I know you're

mad at me, but don't hang up. You don't have to talk to me. I wouldn't have called, but I'm stuck at my Uncle Hendrick's house. It's too icy and I can't get home. I need you to tell my parents I'm spending the night at Uncle Hendrick's. Okay?"

There was a pause. "Okay," said Ruthie. She sounded very far away.

"Wait, Ruthie!" said Kit. "One more thing. I . . . I wanted to say I'm sorry. I'm really sorry."

The line got all crackly and Inky started to bark, so Kit couldn't hear if Ruthie said anything. Finally, Kit hung up.

The room Kit was supposed to sleep in was as cold as a tomb and about as cheery. It had brown wallpaper. The bed was huge, with blankets that were mustard-colored and musty-smelling. They were heavy, but somehow they didn't keep Kit warm, even though she pulled them up to her nose. *If we are evicted from our house and we have to come and live with Uncle Hendrick, will this be my room?* Kit wondered. She shuddered. *I'd rather live in a dungeon.*

For hours, Kit lay stiff and miserable, listening to the ice pelt against the window and the wind rage and the house creak and shift. She thought about all that she was missing at home. By now they would have finished decorating the tree. It probably looked very nice, though Dad wouldn't have put any lights on it. He didn't know they were going to be able to pay the electric bill. A lump rose in Kit's throat.

Just then, she heard scratching at her door. Kit tiptoed across the freezing floor and opened the door a crack. Suddenly, a dark streak bolted across the floor and leaped up onto her bed. It was Inky. Kit climbed back into bed, and Inky curled up next to her. *This has got to be the worst Christmas Eve anyone has ever had!* Kit thought. *No one deserves a Christmas Eve as lonely as this. Not even Inky.* Kit felt so forlorn, she was actually glad for horrible old Inky's smelly, snuffling company. At least he was warm. After a while, Kit fell asleep.

It seemed as if no time at all had passed before a sound woke her. It was the most peculiar thing. Kit was sure she heard jingle bells. She opened her eyes and realized it was morning. Kit got up and pulled the curtains open. At once, the room was flooded with dazzling light. The sun, shining on the dripping, melting ice outside, made prisms of light shimmer on the walls. The sound of the jingle bells was louder. Kit looked out the window, squinting because the bright light was so blinding. She blinked. She couldn't believe what she saw outside on the sidewalk.

Ruthie and Ruthie's father were standing next to their big black car, jingling bells and looking up at the house.

"Ho, ho, ho! Merry Christmas!" shouted Ruthie when she saw Kit's face at the window. "We've come to rescue you! Hurry up and come down!"

Kit rose up on her toes in happiness. "I'll be right there!" she yelled. She'd slept in her clothes, so all she had to do was yank on her shoes before she dashed down the stairs. She flung open the door and ran straight to Ruthie. "Oh, Ruthie!" she said. "I've never been so happy to see anyone in my life! Thank you for helping me!"

Ruthie smiled. "That's what friends are for," she said.

Kit smiled, too. *Friends!* she thought happily.

When Uncle Hendrick was ready, Mr. Smithens drove them all—including Inky—to the Kittredges' house. The roads were slippery, and it was slow going up the hill. Mr. Smithens skidded as he turned into the Kittredges' drive-way, but he pulled the car as close to the house as he could.

The front door flew open. Mother, Dad, Charlie, and all the boarders poured out, calling, "Hurray!" and "Merry Christmas!" and "Kit, we missed you!" When Kit jumped out of the car, everyone tried to hug her at once.

"I'll come back this evening to give you a ride home, sir," Mr. Smithens said to Uncle Hendrick.

Just before she went inside, Kit turned and waved good-bye to Ruthie. "Thanks again! See you later!" she called. "Merry Christmas!"

"Merry Christmas!" Ruthie called back cheerily, waving through the car window.

A merry Christmas it was, too—as merry as any Kit had ever known. Dad surprised Kit with her typewriter, fixed and as good as new, and Charlie gave her a box of typing paper. In the typewriter, there was a piece of paper that said:

```
Fur Kit, Morry Chri tma !
with luvo frum pad and Charlio??
For Kit, Merry Christmas!
with love from Dad and Charlie
```

Mother had a surprise for Kit, too. It was a little black Scottie dog pin. "It was given to me when I was your age," said Mother with a twinkle in her eye. "I thought you might like it. Now that Uncle Hendrick is feeling better, you won't be seeing Inky quite so often."

At the sound of his name, Inky started barking. Kit grinned. "Thanks, Mother," she said, over Inky's ruckus.

But the best surprise by far was Kit's surprise. Kit waited until she and Mother were alone in the kitchen mixing up a batch of waffles.

"We'll eat next to the tree," said Mother. "I'm sure it'll be as lovely as ever, though I *am* sorry we can't have any lights on the tree this year. It just seemed too extravagant, since we can't pay the electric bill."

"Oh yes we can!" said Kit happily. She handed Mother a handkerchief full of coins. "Here's two dollars and forty cents."

Mother looked at the money in disbelief. "Oh my!" she said. "Where did this come from?"

"From Uncle Hendrick," said Kit. "I earned it."

Mother laughed. "Kit Kittredge," she said. "There never was a girl like you! Wait till I tell your father. He'll be just as proud of you as I am." She threw her arms around Kit and hugged her close. "I hope you are proud of yourself, too."

Kit was.

At dusk, Ruthie and her father came back. Kit and Ruthie presented the scarves they had knitted to their fathers, who didn't seem to mind that the scarves had no fringe. After a bit, Mr. Smithens drove Uncle Hendrick and Inky home, and Kit walked Ruthie back to her house.

They were quiet for a little while. Then Kit said, almost shyly, "Uncle Hendrick is all better. Would you . . . would you like to go window-shopping tomorrow?"

"Sure!" said Ruthie.

"The little Scottie pin my mother gave me will look really nice on the collar of your red dress," said Kit. "That is, if you don't mind if I borrow it." It was too dark to see

Ruthie's face, but Kit could tell that she was smiling. Kit went on to say, "That was awfully nice of you to give the ballet tickets to Miss Hart and her boyfriend and Miss Finney and Mr. Peck."

"We can write about their romantic date in our newspaper," said Ruthie, "now that your dad fixed your typewriter. I bet you'll be glad to be writing again. I bet you missed it while you were at your uncle's."

"Well . . ." said Kit. She hesitated and then said, "Ruthie, I have sort of a present for you. It isn't store-bought or anything. But I made it for you. I hope you like it." Kit pulled a thick envelope out of her coat pocket and handed it to Ruthie. "Merry Christmas," she said.

Ruthie opened the envelope and took out Stirling's sketchpad. "The Story of Princess Ruthie," she read aloud from the cover. She looked through the pages. Kit had written a story to go with Stirling's sketches of Ruthie as a princess. "Oh, Kit!" said Ruthie. "Thank you! I know I'll love it. No one ever wrote a book for me before. And one about a princess, too!"

"She's a generous princess," said Kit. "Just like you. In fact, she *is* you. I was thinking of you the whole time I was writing about her."

"This is kind of funny," said Ruthie. "Wait till you see the present my mom and I made for you." Ruthie took a

small package wrapped in tissue paper out
of *her* coat pocket and handed it to Kit.

Kit unwrapped the package. Ruthie's
present was a doll that looked just like Amelia
Earhart! The doll was dressed in a flight cap, jacket, and
gloves just like the ones Amelia Earhart wore in the newsreel, and she had the same eager smile, too.

"Thanks, Ruthie," Kit said. "This is the nicest present
you could possibly have given me. You're a good friend."

"You're a good friend, too," said Ruthie. "I can't wait to
read my princess story. See you tomorrow!"

"Bye," said Kit. "Merry Christmas!"

Kit watched Ruthie run up the driveway and go into
the house. Then she turned around to walk home. When
she saw her own house down the street, she gasped in
surprise.

"Oh, how *beautiful*," she whispered. While she'd been
walking Ruthie home, Dad and Charlie had put the lights
on the Christmas tree. The lights were lit, and through
the window, they glowed as brightly as jewels. Kit stood
in the cold and stared at her family's house, where every
happy Christmas of her life had taken place. *This may be the
last Christmas we'll have in our house*, she thought, feeling a
bittersweet joy. *But it's one I'll never forget. It may even be the
very best Christmas of all.*

*Kit's father had a car dealership like this one—until the Depression forced him to close it.*

The 1920s, before Kit's story begins, were prosperous years. Factories employed millions of workers and cranked out household goods like toasters, toys, clothes, and cars. Then the Depression hit. People lost their jobs and sometimes their life savings. Overnight, middle-class families like Kit's found that they were suddenly poor. Businesses and banks all across the country ran out of money and had to close.

*Sometimes people sold things they owned so they could buy food for their families.*

*Like Stirling's father, these men walked the streets of Chicago looking for work. Sometimes children carried signs, too.*

When Kit's father closed his car dealership because nobody was buying cars, the Kittredges found themselves facing hard times, along with millions of Americans. This financial crisis was so serious that it came to be known as the Great Depression.

Many people had nowhere to turn for help. They felt ashamed to accept free meals at soup kitchens. For most, it was the first time they had to rely on charity. Families and neighbors helped one another as much as they could, but often there was not enough to go around. Like the Kittredges, many families could not pay off debt, such as a home mortgage or car loan, or even pay for essentials like groceries, electricity, or rent.

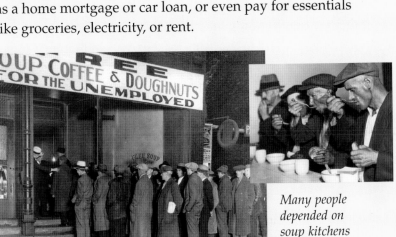

*Many people depended on soup kitchens for their meals.*

In the fall of 1930, the Apple Shippers Association tried to help unemployed workers by selling them crates of apples for $1.75. Thousands of workers began selling apples on the street for five cents each, making a $1.85 profit on each crate. Within weeks, however, the supply of apples ran out—and so did the jobs.

Many children suffered. In West Virginia, a teacher noticed a girl having trouble paying attention during class. When the girl didn't eat at lunchtime, the teacher asked her to run home and get her lunch. She couldn't, the girl explained, because it was Tuesday—her sister's day to eat. Teachers often coordinated food and clothing drives to help students in need, just as Kit's teacher does in the story.

*At food drives, people donated canned goods as well as fresh produce, eggs, cheese, and bread (left). Children who didn't have enough to eat found it hard to pay attention in school (right).*

*To make ends meet, many households took in boarders (left) or laundry (right).*

To save money, many people moved in together. Some turned their homes into boardinghouses, as Kit's family did. But as the Depression deepened, others ended up homeless and started wandering America in search of jobs and food.

People also looked for ways to forget their troubles. Children loved reading comic strips about Little Orphan Annie, who leaves a harsh orphanage for a life of comfort and adventure as the adopted daughter of the wealthy Daddy Warbucks. The beloved comic strip soon became

*Oklahoma farmers were hard hit by years of drought. Many families packed up and moved west, seeking a better life in California.*

*Little Orphan Annie started as a comic strip. She was one of the first pop culture icons to cross over from comics to movies. Her dog, Sandy, was a favorite character, too!*

a popular radio show, and in 1932 it was made into a movie. The story found a new audience when it became a Broadway musical in 1977, with girls playing the roles of Annie and the orphans.

The year 1932, when Kit's story begins, was the lowest point of the Great Depression, and the future looked bleak. President Herbert Hoover did little to provide leadership or government help. He believed that business, if left alone, would correct itself and the Depression would end. But as the hard times got worse, many Americans lost confidence in the president. That November, Franklin Delano Roosevelt was elected to lead the country, beating Hoover by a landslide. Americans were desperate for a change, and they hoped the new president would lead them out of the Depression.

*A rally in support of presidential candidate Franklin D. Roosevelt*

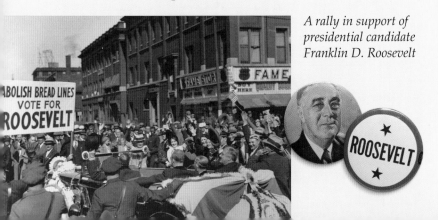

# Turning Things Around

Kit put on a burst of speed. She stretched her arm out, reaching, reaching, reaching for Will's hand. At last, she caught it. Will lifted her up so that she dangled, then swung her so she flew through the air into the boxcar. Kit thudded against the hard wooden floor as she landed.

"Are you okay?" Will asked her.

Kit was too out of breath to talk, so she just nodded. Eagerly, she scrambled to her feet and stood by the open door. The wind blew her hair every which way, smoke stung her eyes, and cinders smudged her face, but she didn't care. Faster and faster the train rushed along the track, until the world outside was just a blur. Kit was exhilarated. She'd never moved so fast! She'd never felt so free! For a second, for a heartbeat, Kit wished the train would never stop.

Then Stirling tugged on her arm. "Kit!" he said urgently. "Lex led us to the wrong train. We're not going north, toward home. We're going south, across the river. Look!"

Kit stuck her head out. Sure enough, the train was barreling across the trestle bridge, the tracks spooling out behind it, the river flowing below. With every click of the wheels, Cincinnati grew smaller and home was farther away.